LEISURE

Kevin Sampson lives and works on Merseyside. His chequered career has embraced the production line at Cadbury's, film production at Channel Four, and the music business front-line of Produce Records, as manager of Liverpool band The Farm. His first novel, *Awaydays*, is being adapted for the screen, and his second, *Powder*, is about a rock group feasting on fame.

Kevin Sampson

LEISURE

VINTAGE

Published by Vintage 2001

2 4 6 8 10 9 7 5 3 1

First published in Great Britain by
Jonathan Cape 2000

Vintage
Random House, 20 Vauxhall Bridge Road,
London SW1V 2SA

Random House Australia (Pty) Limited
20 Alfred Street, Milsons Point, Sydney
New South Wales 2061, Australia

Random House New Zealand Limited
18 Poland Road, Glenfield,
Auckland 10, New Zealand

Random House (Pty) Limited
Endulini, 5A Jubilee Road, Parktown 2193,
South Africa

The Random House Group Limited Reg. No. 954009
www.randomhouse.co.uk

A CIP catalogue record for this book
is available from the British Library

ISBN 0 09 928515 0

Printed and bound in Great Britain by
Bookmarque Ltd, Croydon, Surrey

For my lovely mum – one you can read

The Night Before

Pasternak was having trouble with his yard of ale. Tilting himself further back to guzzle down the last quarter, the fat boy detached the suction of his round cheeks from the mouth of the yard-pipe, allowing beer to trickle out down the sides, down over one chin, over the second and third, streaking out in rivulets over his chest and soaking his T-shirt.

He was ruining his commemorative T-shirt before they even got there. The others had been a bit embarrassed about wearing theirs down to the Waverton Arms tonight, the night before the holiday. Matt had refused from the start, point blank refused to even have one made, but Mikey and Tom were putty in Pastie's hands. He could get them to agree to anything. So there they were in their 'Waverton Arms Drinking Crew Spanish Invasion 2000' shirts. Each had his nickname in felt letters across his shoulders. Mikey was the Inquisitor ('because I like to ask all the questions!'); Tom was Houdini ('there isn't a position I haven't tried!'). And Pasternak? Pasternak, of course, was Doctor Fun – and he was making a good fist of obliterating his pride and joy with a yard of Boddington's.

Matt smiled at his wild-eyed pal, struggling to finish now, struggling to breathe, but still determined to bag that yard of beer. Pasternak was not just his best friend, he was his only friend. The two of them had both been barmen at Flanagan's when they were sixteen. Pasternak was still at school then, Matt newly arrived in the area looking for work. He'd had a notion of coming to Manchester to be near to his mother, but he'd ended up in Stockport, pulling pints. Pasternak was the first person he'd met when he turned up at the bar for his first shift. He'd liked him straight off, from the way he introduced himself as:

'Pasternak. A fat bloke.'

They became good friends, quickly. Pasternak had Matt over to his mum's for Sunday roast and brought him down to the Waverton on their nights off. Matt got on fine with Mikey and Tom, Pasternak's two friends from school, but didn't ever feel especially close to them. Tom was wavy-haired and posh, Mikey was sharp and cynical, always expecting the worst. They were a good laugh. They were successful with girls. Good lads to go out with. And that was about it. They were all off to Spain together tomorrow. It was, as Pasternak would say, going to be a hoot.

He slammed down the yard, gasping for breath, then held up the pipe in triumph.

'Down in one!' he beamed. 'Watch out, España!' He turned to Mikey and Tom. 'Come on, boys! Your turn! Got to get your practice in! From tomorrow, it's for real!'

Meekly, Tom trotted over to humiliate himself. Matt winked at him as he squeezed past, Tom rolling his eyes gamely. Matt watched Pasternak pass over the yard, revelling in his role of master of ceremonies. He loved Pasternak, and there was a mutual respect, too. It was something he'd never quite understood, but Pasternak

2

Day One

Hilary stood in the quietest corner of the airport she could find, issuing final instructions to Becky, things she'd forgotten to note down on her list of things to remember. Becky'd be fine. She'd have no problems running the spa. But still, it was a worry. It was bound to be, leaving a business she'd built up single-handedly, a business that was thriving but was now also suffering imitators all over the city. Hilary's had been the first alternative remedies spa in Chester, and she still offered the widest choice of philosophies – to Hilary the methods she sold were more than mere treatments. They were lifestyles. Philosophies.

She'd built up a loyal client base and a small team of skilled and motivated therapists, but it seemed as though each week brought the opening of a new salon offering Indian head massage, acupressure, Alexander technique. No one else was offering Pilates at the moment, but Hilary felt the pervasive and overbearing gloom of a faceless threat. She couldn't have chosen a worse time to go away, but how could she have known that when she booked? It was only a couple of months ago, and had she not had this holiday to anticipate, to relish, to bloody well cling to as her marriage lurched toward the point of no respite then she could have seen herself just asking him to leave. There was no logic to it, no rationale – she was just *tired* of Shaun.

She was glad that she'd ridden out the crisis. Switching off the mobile now, determined not to look at it again for seven whole days, she allowed the notion that perhaps she had not been truly there for Shaun after the accident. But then, running the argument around her head like a dentist's mouthwash, she spat it out with the same conviction as always. Nonsense. She had been nothing less than a rock to that man. She had been everything to him. Nurse, cook, cleaner, guide, sounding board for his increasingly deranged plans – Hilary had *been* there. She'd been everything except his lover, and that was just something they'd both got used to. It wasn't her fault.

She didn't even mind so much, especially as the months raced on. In the absence of Shaun's wage she had at last acted upon her growing instinct that those recreational interests with which she filled her day – t'ai chi, massage, Pilates, natural healing – could form the basis of a business. What she missed in physical love from her husband was compensated for by the thrill of a new beginning. It was a new life for her, all but.

She could see Shaun, making his way out of Boots with the goodies that, with their flight delayed three hours, would now form an early lunch. For a second she was jolted by a visceral yearning for him. What *was* that? It was sexual, certainly, for she felt that snatched sighting of him in her loins just as though it was the first time again. She longed for him, but there followed another wave immediately afterwards, something more akin to compassion. Was it pity? It was as though her yin and her yang were fighting back conflicting emotions. Why would anyone pity a man who looked like that?

Because of his earpiece, perhaps – that full-sized hearing aid he insisted on wearing like a scarlet letter.

She watched him gazing around the concourse trying to pick her out, unaware, as always, of the effect he had on women. They were actually nudging each other to make sure their companions had not missed the treat. 'Jesus', his workmates at the cathedral used to call him. In the five years she'd known him he'd been compared to Pat Cash, Brad Pitt, even Kurt Cobain. He had Cobain's dishevelled hair, his dirty-blond beard and those stunning ice-blue eyes, but Kurt was a dwarf. Shaun Hughes was six foot three and a magnificent specimen to behold. He was slim and graceful, walking with the understated pride and easy athleticism of those gifted with a supple and powerful physique. Hilary remembered well the first time she'd unbuttoned his shirt. She'd let out a stifled yelp at, not so much the sight of his strong chest, but the *extent* of it. It was broad and taut, tanned from all those years working outdoors and covered with a faint golden down. Hilary was captivated, entranced that a man could be this beautiful. She'd kissed his chest, gently, all over, then lain her head on it, not quite able to take in that this was to be hers, all hers.

With his long hair and his muscles and his silent, prowling presence she called him Leonidas – but the stonemasons were right, too. He was Jesus. When he fell thirty feet from the cathedral gable he was restoring, they all came to visit him in hospital, then less so, and after six months he was pensioned off and no one really bothered much about Jesus after that. The pension was a pittance. He was fine, but the way the fall had affected his eyes meant that he'd never be allowed to go up a ladder or work on a gantry again. It took a while for the full implications of that to sink in with him and during that time, the worst period, she'd given nothing but support and tact and sympathy. All she seemed to do was listen and nod and encourage him. Yet he seemed determined to have a life apart from her, to not need her.

In retrospect, Hilary could say that Shaun had always been antiquated. When they'd first started going out, she loved his decisive conservatism. He seemed so sophisticated and she so gauche. She was ever conscious of the age difference in those days – she was just twenty-five now, Shaun thirty-six. If anything he seemed to have grown younger, but only in a childish way. He was *petty*. He was a snob. He seemed to disapprove of everything – television, McDonald's, football, computers and especially her mobile phone. He made a face every time it rang, every time she used it. She was glad to get out of the house in the morning.

She'd tried to be interested in all his barmy plans. He was going to set up a charitable trust, to do the work English Heritage couldn't take on. Then he was going to set himself up as a special consultant working alongside architects on major renovation projects. Nothing came of any of his schemes. He ended up cutting stone to size in a salvage yard. That was when his behaviour really started to worry Hilary. He would just go missing, without telling her where he was going. He'd be gone all day then show up last thing at night, silent, defying her to enquire. She was worried at first, troubled that he was showing all the signs of depression. But when he dead-batted all her questions, she started to wean herself off. She stopped caring. She found that she liked having time to herself. It was a relief. So when Shaun started taking those night-time walks, she just didn't want to know. She couldn't even be bothered trying to guess. Nothing would surprise her, though she doubted he was up to anything sinister.

When she was twenty, Shaun was everything she could have imagined wanting – creative, sensitive, laid-back, strong – and he looked like a god. She would lie with her head on his chest, asking questions about him. She wanted to know about everything he'd ever done, every incident, all that made him the man she was falling in love with. So what happened? Only this. She'd become so used to not needing him that it didn't seem unusual for her husband to have a secret life. Or a secret compartment in his life, such as it was, at least. The only thing that hurt, if she ever thought about it, was how little it bothered her now.

She watched him picking his way through the crowds with their eager faces and their high hopes. It was all so random. People heading off in high excitement to places they'd picked out of an airbrushed brochure. The lucky dip of the holiday market was as random as their choice of partner – and as likely to succeed. How on earth did she come to be married to Shaun, just six months after meeting him? What set of circumstances had led up to it, and made her believe that this was the way for her? She'd been in love, of course. Totally and madly in love with a man she barely knew then and didn't know now. She waved to make sure he'd seen her.

The accident had robbed Shaun of his self-certitude, but the only outward sign of any injury was a head tilted minutely backwards from months in a neck brace. That, and those staring eyes, like a collie being examined by the vet. She hated the cast that gave to his lovely face. She could not get used to it. And the hearing aid. He could have had a microscopic one, invisible to the eye, but it was as though he wanted to embarrass people, make them acknowledge his plight. Girls in lycra eyed him as he surveyed the Departures forecourt, flicking looks at his bum and his thighs and his dick. He was crumpet all right, Shaun. As he located Hilary, smiled minimally and made his way towards her, she watched him with mixed emotions. This was her man, after all. Maybe she could have taken more trouble to find out what was going on with him. She was glad they were going to have this time together. Maybe they could work it all out over there, under the sun, away from it all. One way or another, she hoped the holiday would give her a clue.

Pasternak was insistent.

'What else is there to do in an airport for three hours?'

'We'll be drunk before we get there!'

'We'll be thrown off the plane! That's routine, now!'

'Don't be gay! That's just *gay* talk, that is! Come on – everyone to the bar!'

They dragged themselves after their portly leader.

'Hey, I didn't tell you! You can get Viagra over the counter in Spain. So I'm told anyway.'

'What good's that going to be to you, you virgin?'

'He can always use it on Pam!'

'Who's Pam?'

'Pam of his hand!'

They groaned and trooped into the bar.

★

12

Shaun spotted his wife and made his way slowly towards her. She deserved this break, Hilary. It wasn't his idea of a holiday, a resort complex with pool and bar and fellow tourists you'd have to nod to, but it was what she wanted. She'd been through a lot these past couple of years. It was easy to forget how hard the crisis had hit her, too. She'd been shaken inside out, then asked to pick up the pieces. He'd never pressurised her about anything – money, mortgage, sex – but Shaun knew well how keenly she'd felt it and how deeply she was affected. It was easy, too, to forget how young she still was, and that made him weep for her even more.

He did that a lot, these days. Not out of self-pity – it just felt good. It was a release. Often, after he'd been out butchering plaster Zeus fountains, he'd sit down in a quiet place and cry. He knew he disappointed her. He knew she was slipping away from him. He couldn't do anything about it. It was what it was.

He disappointed himself, too. He was nothing. His had been the most intricate of apprenticeships – *apprenticeship*! Do they have those, now? It had taken him eleven years in all to become a master stonemason. Now he was nothing. No longer a mason, no longer a man.

He picked his way through the crowds awaiting their flights. Their *flights*. Their great escape from routine, from drudgery, from depression, from normality. These people, for a short time, wanted to behave as abnormally as possible. This, for them, was what the past few months had been all about. The anticipation of a week or two in a place which was much hotter than the places they lived. It was somewhere else and being somewhere else was going to solve all the ills of their mundane

13

existences. So, what did they think? These little piglets from Leigh and Widnes and Nantwich, all congregated together in nervous, excited gaggles. Did they think that when they got off the plane at Malaga they'd be transformed? They'd just suddenly become objects of intrigue? He wanted to tell them that it wasn't going to happen for them. They'd get pink, they'd get pissed, but that was it. The sun wasn't going to melt their problems away – or their fat legs, for that. He sighed deeply. He was no better himself. He was worse. A cripple, incapable of seeing the light, unable even to have fun.

He caught Hilary's eye and smiled. What did it for him every time, even after all these years, was the immediate word association on sight of her petite frame and short hair and fiery brown eyes. *Elfin*. She hated the incipient patronage of that word, but preferred anything to *pixieish*. Shaun smiled at the thought. She was a lovely girl. He had to make this holiday work for her.

And he *was* looking forward to it. When he'd first realised that their resort, Nerja, was within shot of so much glorious history – the Alhambra Palace, Antequera, even old Malaga itself – Shaun had been almost coltish. That was before Hilary pointed out that she had no intention of spending her first week off in ages trudging around dank old buildings. She wanted nothing more or less than some lazy days by the pool or on the beach, reading, wallowing, doing nothing much at all. They'd compromised on one day trip to an ancient site of his choice, after which he was welcome to go on as many organised coach tours as he could cram in – without her.

'Get everything?' she smiled.

'And more.'

'Ooh – a mystery! What is it?'

'*Low-fat* Cheddar-and-chive crisps!'

'No!'

'Oh yes, m'dear. And sarsparilla. Real sarsparilla!'

'My God! I can't wait!'

They headed off to a vacant seat. They were getting on. It was all going to be fine.

Because of the extra space he desired more than required, Shaun had ticked the physical disability box on the booking form and answered a few questions over the telephone. The outcome was that he was now sitting in whole acres of legroom, splendidly convenient for the exit and directly opposite two friendly stewardesses who seemed not just ready but keen to cater to his physically-impaired needs. He felt a spasm of guilt at their eager, attentive jollity and wondered what they'd think when he sprinted off this plane the moment the go-ahead was given, but such thoughts flitted rather than hovered.

Besides, he was a model patient compared to the decrepit old bastard they'd wheeled in next to him. Actually wheeled him in, coughing and wheezing, and dumped him into the seat next to Shaun. Shaun made no attempt to make eye contact or conversation. That would've been crazy. They hadn't even taken off yet.

As he sat there, starting to shiver in the icy blast of the cabin's air-conditioning, Shaun felt sure that the old corpse had farted. An all-consuming, deadly rotten smog enveloped them, so rancid that it almost seemed to smell green. He couldn't help but sniff at it, as though convincing himself that it was as bad as he thought. He eyed the stewardesses wildly, but they seemed to notice neither the smell nor the madman trying to get their attention. They were strapping in. The plane was taking off. Of course – that would be it. Start-up smells, engine fluids, general take-off pong – that's what the smell was. Sitting here, they were probably right above the nerve centre of it all. The on-board crew wouldn't notice a thing – they'd be used to the hum by now.

They got up above the silver-grey whip of cloud and everything seemed to settle down. There was no more smell. The old boy set about getting his fair share of attention without delay. Exercising the right of the repulsive living dead to badger, berate, demand and complain, his knotted fingers were on the buzzer immediately the 'fasten seatbelts' light went off. He'd spent a moment trying to enlist Shaun's help with a series of prods and phlegm-enhanced croaks, but Shaun was having none of it. He pretended to be asleep.

The rattling man summoned a bright, chatty steward and convinced him that he'd need two miniatures of brandy right away. The camp steward patronised him with a 'you old devil – whatever shall we do with you!' stance and spun off to get the drinks.

'Bloody queer!' rasped the geriatric. Shaun dozed with yet more conviction.

The brandies seemed to do the trick. It was within a minute of hearing him slurp and suck at his first brandy-and-ice that the stench returned. This time it was worse. It was poisonous. Shaun felt himself blanketed, suffocating under a pall of rank, yellow-green gas. He coughed and took advantage of affecting to wake up by snatching up his in-flight magazine and wafting theatrically at the smell.

'Jesus! What's that!'

It was the old man's turn to ignore him. He didn't give a toss, of course, but he wasn't going to own up to it. He was a master polluter. A few minutes later he slipped another one out. This time the stewardesses, who were starting to prepare meals, looked over in distress.

'Shit!' thought Shaun. 'They think it's me!'

To counter any such notions he wafted gently with his laminated safety procedure card, pulling disgusted faces to himself so that any observer would know that it was not he who dunnit.

Prrrrrp!

A wet, slithery fart preceded that same cancerous stench. That was enough. Shaun stood up. For just that precise moment he felt he was going to say something to the old bastard.

'I don't know why you can't just go to the toilet.'

That's what he would have liked to say. But he stayed silent. He made a pleading face at the steward, shrugged and got up out of his seat. He went to find Hilary and killed time hanging over her, embarrassing her with news of the farting man.

'Always the last bloody bag to come out! I bet you it's on its way to Cyprus or somewhere! Why's it always us?'

'There's lots of people still waiting for their bags. Look!'

She glanced around. He was right. Dozens of people were loitering around the now barren carousel, no one owning up to the baby buggy and the parasol, which had been drearily circulating for a quarter of an hour.

'It was a busy flight. They've probably just unloaded the plane in two lots.'

'Trust us to be in the second lot!'

'As opposed to what? Sweltering on a baking hot coach that can't move until everyone's on board? We're better off here, love. The coach's air-conditioning can't work until the driver starts the engine, you know?'

Don't call me love, she hissed to herself. *Do not call me love!*

He tried to massage her shoulders. She dropped her handbag to the floor and squared up to him.

'Listen. If you're going to be a know-all for the rest of the holiday we may as well get on separate coaches . . .'

He smiled and continued rubbing her neck. 'You need time to adjust. Try and unwind.'

She picked up her bag, wishing she knew why his patience always irked her so.

'I thought you said we were going to Marbella!' Mikey glowered at Pasternak.

'I *mentioned* Marbella, Mikey, I merely mentioned it. Marbella was just one of many resorts we might have been allocated . . .'

'Yeah, fucking allocated on arrival! You never mentioned that bit, either! We'll probably be sent to some dump, miles away from the beach, shit resort, no tot, no clubs, fuck all! Shit! Why did we ever listen to you, Plastic Man? We could be in Ibiza now!'

Tom cleared his throat.

'Where *is* Nerja, anyway?'

'Precisely.'

They hauled their bags to coach number 17.

★

The boys were disappointed when the travel rep hopped on board. Sitting at the back of the coach, they'd slavered and ogled a whole chapter of resort agents in bright miniskirts, all sharing tips and gossip in the shade. The Sunflight girls looked gorgeous from what the Waverton Arms Drinking Crew could see of them. Maybe this'd be an early opportunity to strike. But when Davina hauled herself up on to the bus and gave the all-clear to set off, their hopes were punctured. She was thickset and bespectacled. Not that the specs were a turn-off in themselves, but behind the brick-thick lenses hid the confused, convulsive eyes of a someone who'd become used to life happening to her. She wasn't going to be much fun, Davina.

Her commentary, as they travelled, confirmed as much. She came across like a supply teacher, someone trying to inspire confidence and show authority but who, importantly, had forgotten to convince herself first. Her mantra, which she dearly hoped would give all on board a crash course in Costa del Sol essentials, faded into the background as weary holidaymakers tuned out to watch the scenery go by.

'What I always say about a Spanish sun is treat it with respect. Yeah? I'm a great believer in what I like to call temperance. I'm a firm believer in too much on the first day can ruin the rest of your holiday. And that applies to what I like to call the whole caboodle.'

Only Pasternak laughed. He laughed and laughed – he found her spectacularly amusing. 'Excellent!'

Davina pressed on. 'Tomorrow morning I'll be hosting what we think of as . . .' She did inverted commas with her fingers. 'An "informal get-together" by the pool bar where I can run through some of the trips and outings we have available to you at some very special prices. Yeah? And the informal get-together is, of course, a great opportunity to meet your fellow travellers.'

Shaun winced at the thought and tensed his wrists. Hilary stared out of the window, still swooning from her brief eye contact with one of the young lads at the back of the coach. What a stunner! She felt a pang of envy for the lucky girl who was going to get off with him during the holiday.

'Now, I'm a great believer in really just easing yourselves into your first day on holiday, which is why I'm holding the informal get-together by the pool at eleven o'clock, for all you sleepyheads who fancy a lie-in. Remember it's your first day, and remember it's HOT out here, yeah? What I always say about your first day is –' She paused to give added impact to what they were about to receive. ' – Take it easy. Yeah? Have a *smashing* holiday.'

Pasternak applauded generously, jerking Shaun, three rows ahead, out of his reverie. He'd been lost in the grave, ochre sierras. The grandeur of them, their scale, settled his spirit, taking him right back to his youth. The outdoors, field trips, mountains in particular gave him an animal joy, a sense of his own difference that even back then, he thought, marked him out as someone who would work with nature's materials. He was starting to feel good already. All that anger and frustration was ebbing away with each dramatic bend of the road and the stunning new mountain vistas beyond.

In those first months after he'd finally shed the neck brace, he'd returned to the big outdoors to try to recapture some of that rampant, hopeful liberty of his boyhood. It seemed that he might not work again as a stonemason – not in the way he'd known before, for certain. The word had been passed around that Shaun's eyes and his unsteady hand would no longer be capable of the intricate stonework at which he specialised. He turned up for a job at Chirk Castle one day soon after and he knew straight away from the nervous pacing and the lowered eyeline of the site manager that something had been said.

Then came the worst part, working at an architectural salvage yard where he'd dress chunks of stone into usable blocks and slabs. He hated it. It was butchery. He was being asked to reduce ornately carved sandstone gateposts to plain, reusable blockstones. They paid him four pounds an hour on twenty-four hours' notice and sold the reclaimed stone for eighty pounds a yard. He could have stuck it out for the occasional treasures he was asked to restore, jobs he tackled with the patient, loving eye of the master craftsman. But even these rare treats left him angry and bewildered. A project that took him four weeks of painstaking work, blasting, matching, carving, engraving and paid him just over £600, was immediately sold on for a shade under five grand. He started to hate the clients as much as his employers, two spivs who'd give cowboys a bad name. He walked out when the younger boss asked him to cut the base off a marble bust, possibly Augustan, for a customer in St Helen's who wanted to cement it to his swimming pool wall.

'That's it, Shaun, matey,' he muttered to himself as he waited for the bus that day. 'That's your fucking lot.'

So he'd headed for the hills. Only as far as the bus or the train would take him in a day – Moel Famau,

Snowdonia, the Cambrians, the Peak District – and always to places he could climb up and look down from. These were the days when he found peace with his soul. There was always regret, too, but he found sweet solace in his long walks. Out there, out here, the somnolent magnificence of these ancient ranges was soothing him again, filling him up. He'd climb one of these mountains, one day this week. He'd sit up on top of it and gaze down at the tiny world below and feel good.

Someone behind started clapping, bringing Shaun back from his reverie. One by one, two by two, most of the other passengers added their applause. Davina's surprised eyes were moist with happiness.

Shaun didn't know who he was angriest at – Hilary, the hunchback who'd carried the bags or himself for letting him. A porter was the last thing he'd expected in an apartment complex like this. He'd just appeared from nowhere as the keys were being handed over, grabbed three bags in one hairy hand and flung another holdall over his shoulder as though it were a beanbag. He'd grunted for them to follow him and half jogged down the succession of steps and ornamental pathways that led to their own villa, each tough knuckle straining against the weight of the luggage.

He grunted again and held out his hand for the key when they got there, sweating madly, a couple of minutes later. He ran a sly eye over Shaun as he groped for the key, then wiped his hand on a pot-bellied T-shirt before letting them into the apartment. Then he stood there. And continued to stand there.

Hilary eyed Shaun frantically, making embarrassed

gestures with her head. Shaun looked at the little guy, puzzled. His expression seemed to be saying:

'You're a big man, sure, but I carried all your bags in *one hand*! And your lady – she *likes* that! She likes how strong I am!'

Hilary cleared her throat.

'Have you got something for him, then?'

Shit! A tip! The chap wanted paying, of course. Shaun hadn't changed any traveller's cheques yet. All he had was a 100 peseta coin (too little; about 30p) and a 5,000 note (way too much). He turned his back on the guy and rooted through his pockets self-consciously. Fuck. Fuck! He was going to have to give him the note! Fifteen quid for carrying bags he hadn't even asked to be carried! Fuck! Meekly, he handed over the money, an inane grin frozen on his gritted teeth. The bloke didn't even say *gracias*. He thought Shaun was a pansy. He closed the door after him and flopped down on the bed, trying to find a funny side to it.

'Two-bedroom apartment for family of six. One-bedroom flat for party of four.'

'No. No. Listen. I specifically requested a *two*-bedroom facility. I physically, actually specified it, wrote it down, *paid* for it!'

'Two-bedroom apartment for family of six. You, party of four.'

Pasternak knew that to raise his voice, to rise to temper would destroy any remote chance they had of getting the accommodation they'd requested. He tried to stay pleasant.

'It's a simple administrative glitch. Why don't you fax

the tour operator and they'll confirm what I've just told you?'

'No. You don't wasting no more my time.'

He produced the keys with a dismissive flick.

'Flat 412. Passport.'

'What?'

'Four passport.'

'Why?'

'No passport, no key.'

'But – do you really need *all* our passports?'

The only variation was a slight, impatient beckoning with his right hand.

'Four passport. 20,000 pesetas.'

'*What?*'

'Deposit.'

Pasternak had him.

'How can we change traveller's cheques without our passports?'

'Change here.'

'Hah! I don't really think so, *matey*!'

The diminutive proprietor scrutinised Pasternak with tiny black eyes, touched his moustache with the tip of his tongue and nodded minutely.

'Three passport. 20,000 pesetas.'

Pasternak couldn't be bothered arguing. This was valuable drinking time they were wasting. He rounded up the passports, broke the news about the apartment, took the barbs from Mikey and wondered to himself whether now, at last, the fun would start.

'What time is it?'

'Half four.'

'Cripes. It's hot for half four, isn't it?'

'Stifling.'

'What d'you want to do?'

'Dunno. Might be a nice time of day just to slob out by the pool. Get a bit of a base tan while the sun's not so savage.' She eyed him with mischief. 'Meet some of the other holidaymakers.'

Shaun twitched. He was about to offer up a defence when Hilary laughed.

'Gotcha!'

He held up a hand in defeat, but kept his worried expression.

'Seriously, though! Don't so much as even catch anybody's eye, all right? I know you. You'll get us lumbered. Too scared of giving offence.'

'ME! Who is it who has to make a prize idiot of himself trying to talk in French, or Greek or Spanish?'

'That's just good manners. You shouldn't just assume that everyone automatically speaks English . . .'

She cackled wickedly. '*Dar*-ling! We're in Spain! In a resort! Of course they speak English!'

'Nonetheless . . .'

'Bollocks!'

'It's nice to just show a bit of willing . . .'

'Bollocks!'

'At least at first!'

She beamed at him, enjoying a rare supremacy.

'Utter cack, and you know it!' She went for the jugular. 'And what about all those dishes you can never actually bring yourself to eat. It's like school dinners. You end up hiding half of it under your napkin.'

'Do not.'

'Do too.' She squealed in delight. 'What about Crete? The sheep's head!'

She clapped her hands. He was annoyed. She could tell from his super-solemn, patient expression.

'Look, same principle. It may not matter to you caring spiritual types . . .'

'Ooooooh!'

'But I take the view that it's just plain . . . *nice* to try and meet the locals halfway. We're in *their* country – we're not here to ride roughshod all over them and their culture . . .'

'No, we're here to bail out their national debt!'

'Oh, stop it! You know you don't mean that . . .'

'I bloody do! And I'm going to speak English all week and if they don't bloody well understand me they're not going to earn much bunce, are they?'

She was alive with naughtiness, spoiling for a row. For a second their eyes locked, hers sparkling, taunting him. The strap of her vest had fallen across her shoulder, hinting at the lively breasts below, those small tits he used to love to suck and feel. He should just go across and kiss her, see where that would lead. But he wasn't sure. They'd only just arrived. It was early days. He might blow it if he tried too soon. He peeled off his shorts right there in front of her, letting his semi swing out as he rummaged for his Speedo's. He stepped into them, knowing she was watching him.

'Fancy a swim?'

A moment of understanding passed between them and with that look a truce was called.

Shaun paid for two sun loungers and went to select the newest from the stack in the corner of the pool's patio. As he inspected them, three assistants of varying age and size materialised from a cabin and started fighting to help him carry his sunbeds the ten paces to where he'd left the towels. With ingratiating grins and ever more desperate tugs, they tried to interest him in this lounger and that cushion, all of which looked indentical and quite uncomfortable. News of the Big Tipper had spread fast. He was going to have to disappoint them and carry his own. He was determined to work off a week's worth of gratuities with unnecessary toil.

'Hey! Muzzy Man was right! This place is fine!'

And it was. With its marble floor, generous and well-proportioned rooms and good-sized sofa bed, the boys' apartment could have been a lot worse. Pasternak yanked open the fridge.

'Look! A welcome pack!'

'It's the last lot's leftovers, Plastic-ass!'

'It's not! Orange juice, water, bread rolls . . .'

He snatched them up and flopped on to the sofa, forcing bread and orange juice down his gullet simultaneously.

'Superb!'

He looked all around him, gulping down the food, talking with his mouth full.

'This is going to be great! This place is going to be transformed into . . . The Love Pad!'

Mikey tossed his curls. 'And in the highly unlikely event of you failing to pull, which one of us lucky guys gets to sleep in your slipstream?'

'Well, I dunno, guys. Guess you're going to have to toss for that one.'

Matt smiled and winked at him. Pasternak grinned back.

'Come on! Let's go let the babes know we're HEE-YAH!'

He drummed on his chest with his fists and ran for the door. No one followed.

Shaun kept his eyes tight shut. Standing in the pool, mere feet from where he lay, a Been Here Before was jousting with a Leaving Tomorrow. Amazingly, they seemed to be enjoying each other's conversation, both confirming that the highlights of the Costa del Sol were, indeed, the absolute highlights of the Costa del Sol.

'I mean, you've got to see a bullfight, haven't you, just to say you've been?'

'Course you have.'

'I mean, just so that you have that opinion.'

'Yes.'

Pause.

'Did you do Gib?'

'Oh, fantastic. Wouldn't have missed it for the world.'

'The monkeys!'

'Uh-huh! And Marks, as well!'

'Mandy didn't fancy it, mind.'

'Marks and Spencer?'

'The bullfighting. I had to do that one on my own.'

Shaun doubted whether either of the young bores had been at all. Not yet forty and talking like old bastards. There was a certain acceptance, an equilibrium between their facile chatter and their comfortable tummies that, he was sure, would allow them to stand there, in the shallow end, agreeing with each other until their hair fell out.

'We come here every year, now.'

'We were just saying that last night. We're off home tomorrow morning, but we'd definitely book again. Definitely.'

'Well, this is it. I mean, once you find somewhere you like and you get to know it that bit better, why take that risk?'

Quick as a flash, before the other chap could concur or demur, he drove home the advantage of several seasons under this Andalusian sky.

'Done Frigiliana?'

'Going tonight.'

'Ah. Got to do Frigiliana. Haven't done the Costa 'til you've done Frig.'

Shaun was seething. The bloke had just said he was going tonight! What was up with these people? It was bad enough when two like this pair, each a master of mediocrity, colluded in their own pacts of moribundity. But what if, as was their real wont, they hung around the pool until a tiddler swam into their sights. A New Boy? Someone upon whom they could foist any number of self-regarding opinions and advice, solicited or not. If they stood there long enough some poor fool would catch their eye and that would be that.

'Been here long?'

'Just arrived today, actually.'

'Really? Tell you something for nothing, mate. Avoid Seville. Avoid Seville like the fucking plague. Nothing there. Fucking dump.'

A distant and reassuring slap of the pool's surface broke into his subconscious and burgled his attention. Hilary! Shit! She was in the pool. If those two bores started talking to her he was bound to get roped in himself. She'd do it out of perversity, call him over and

29

introduce him. He sneaked a look from behind his shades. Out of harm's way for now. She was sticking to laps on the other side of the pool. But it could all change at any time. Any moment now either of them would suddenly notice her, realise that this was some-one who they had not yet obliged with the benefit of their knowledge. The sudden impact of loud, coarse voices made him sit up.

'WOY-HOY!'

'DARREN, MOY SAN!'

A skinhead in the pool waved.

'WOY-HOY, MOY SAN!'

Three pasty young men ran towards the pool, tits jiggling.

'CAMMIN ATCHA, YOU KANT!'

A blur of bald heads and vast, checked swimming shorts then – SPLOSH! He was soaked. That was it. Shaun was off for a walk.

They padded across the Balcón Europa, ice creams in hand.

'Can't see many clubs, Pastie!'

'Well, they don't have them in the town centre, do they?'

'What? Run that one by me again! They don't have clubs in the town centre? Where the fuck do they have them, then? The suburbs?'

'Sort of, yeah. They have them out on the periphery, so that people like us can make as much noise as we want.'

Mikey looked unconvinced. Tom, silent until now, piped up. 'Forget the clubs. I can't see too many bloody *girls*!'

'I can't see *any*!'

Pasternak laughed and stopped where he was outside the Irish bar.

'Whoa! Hold on, boys, hold on! Two things. One. If, at the end of this holiday, you have failed to come in the mouth of a hot Latino babe then I will personally refund your money. And two. Get off my back about Ibiza, will you? We're not there. We're here. Let's make the most of it!'

Matt nodded. Mikey leaned over him. 'But whose idea was it to come here, hey? Not mine. I don't get you. With all the fucking money you're on, you choose a late-availability, allocate-on-arrival, cheapo special when you could be larging it in San An! What's with you?'

Pasternak spread his arms out wide. 'I just can't pass up a bargain. Sorry, guys, but it's going to be fantastic. You'll see.'

'Or our money back, yeah?'

'Won't come to that.'

'What if we get off with a couple of blondes from Barnsley?'

'Latino was a figure of speech.'

Mikey was elated. 'No way, man! You've said it now! No horn-mad señorita, no payee holiday!'

They reached what seemed like a dead end.

'Hold on,' said Matt. He strolled over to the balustrade. Below, steps hewn out of the rock face led down to a cliff-side café. And sitting outside the café were three girls.

'Er, chaps. Over here a mo.'

Hilary didn't know whether she should feel pleased, or

defensive or angry or what. She'd been at the other end of the pool, tried to call out to Shaun to see where he was going, then hauled herself out and thought: 'Sod it. I'll doze in the sun for half an hour. Can't hurt me too much at this time of day.' So she found a little patch of grass next to the pool, spread her towel and stretched out, ready to let the caressing sunshine take her off to a land of no cares. And then she heard them, two female voices, young, but one of them hoarse from smoking or shouting or both.

'Did you see the lash on that bloke?'

There was a note of prurient thrill in her voice.

'See it? I nearly tripped over it!'

'Fuckinell! It weren't real!'

'Imagine having that up you!'

'I am doing!'

They both guffawed and set into a bout of bawdy speculation about the man who was her husband. Specifically, they indulged in lusty and vivid fantasy about the splendour of his cock. It was too late to tell the girls to shut up and besides, it was true. Shaun had a huge knob, a fact that those ludicrous old-fashioned swimming briefs he still wore did nothing to conceal. What Hilary wanted to tell them was that his penis was actually beautiful, too. It always seemed radiant to her, effulgent and clean of line – nothing like the gnarled instruments of torture that other girls used to warn of. She'd seen three in her life, one of which was connected to her father, the other belonging to Sam, her young brother. Shaun's was nothing like either of theirs. It was a splendid, big, shining thing, Shaun's penis.

At least, that's how she used to feel. When she'd first

started going out with him in her last year at uni, tipsy and pleased to be finally joining in a conversation like that, she'd made the mistake of telling her friends about his prodigious cock, with the result that one after another of them threw themselves at Shaun over the ensuing weeks. He amiably and firmly rebuffed each lunge. How mightily had she adored him back then? What a headspin, what a mind-blowing few months that had been. It was not so very long ago. Lying there now, the sun easing her tense brow, she hadn't a cohesive idea how she felt about him, or anything about the two of them together, and she couldn't be bothered thinking it through.

He felt better and better, the further he walked. The gardens leading down to the lake at the bottom of the resort tumbled with mimosa, vulgar red rasping orchids, lime and peach trees and squat, miniature yuccas like great, patient pineapples. He traipsed along the brick-work paths, breathing in the suffusion of aromas, the top notes of bougainvillea and the erotic choke of lilies, meandering down and round and down again. Darting glass-green lizards shot out in front of him, hesitated, blinking from wise compound eyes, then scuttled for the shade of the rockery. Shaun waited quietly by the scorched red clay borders, hoping for another sight of the gecko. He could feel it watching him, waiting for him to go. He moved on down the pathway, stopping to take in the small lagoon as it opened out below him.

The water level had fallen already, a result of the unrelenting sun. Decadent lilies congregated on the shadowy surface of the nearest, south-western expanse and as Shaun crouched to dip his fingers in the water his eye was taken by a slight, sudden motion. Kneeling closer he saw that almost every leaf was occupied by a tiny frog, no bigger than a half of his thumb. The frogs stayed utterly still for a minute, two minutes, then leaped for some invisible fly or a better vantage point.

Gliding below with a slovenly grace was a carp, prowling and waiting for any lapse in the frogs' concentration. Shaun sat back against a pillar of random stone, happy to watch the lazy pond-life. He could feel himself being taken over by the gradual swooning euphoria he used to feel on his childhood vacations. It would only be Anglesey or Colwyn Bay, the car journey would take hour after stifling hour, but when they finally got there Shaun would run and run until he was exhausted and even then his mounting rapture would make him want to carry on running and laughing. This holiday was going to be perfect. A good bowl of real Andalusian gazpacho followed by wood-grilled catch of the day and a good night's kip and Shaun Scanlon would be ready for the hidden churches and villages of the high sierras.

The three girls were from Nijmegen and, Pasternak was delighted to discover, tremendous fun. The two blondes, Anke and Krista, were pure MTV babes, tall, stunning-looking girls but not remotely haughty about it. They'd giggled at his foolish introduction.

'Ladies, Doctor Fun is delighted to make your acquaintance! That's me. Pasternak. The chap with the big personality.'

They actually seemed to like him, although their eyes darted surreptitiously all over the other three. No matter. The third girl, the brunette, Millie, seemed positively captivated by him. She had a round face, pretty with big eyes and a perfect, short, glossy bob that stayed still when she laughed. She laughed at everything he said, showing the glint of a stud in her tongue. *And* she was a little on the hefty side. He was in!

They'd all sat there in the bar overlooking the beach drinking happy hour cocktails with salacious names and vicious colours. Pasternak flirted with Millie.

'May I interest ma'am in a Slow Comfortable Screw?'

'Only if sir will accept a Pussy Galore!'

They whiled away an innocent hour comparing tattoos and pierced navels, giving each other the chance to inspect the goods at close quarters. Pasternak's guess, from the way he caught both Anke and Krista lingering over his flat brown stomach, was that Matt would be having to make his choice sooner than the rest of them. Bastard! Even his ribcage was walled with muscle.

The girls produced a pre-wrapped, conical spliff from their purse, and sparked up the fresh, instantly potent grass. They spoke that near-perfect, Californian-tinged English of all Northern Europeans. Krista was laughing about some of the guys they'd met a few days before, reliving some of the choice chat-up lines, when Pasternak put on his best Lancashire accent, pushed out his impressive gut, strummed it with the tips of his fingers and said: 'It's all beer, is this! All bloody beer!'

The girls were silent for a second then fell about laughing. Emboldened, he looked them up and down and started rambling in the same Ecky Thump accent.

'Ay though, ay? Know what they say about you Dutch girls! Ay! Kerr-nudge, kerr-nudge, ah-wink, ah-wink, ay? No smoke without fire!'

Tom turned his seat to face the other way. Mikey put

his head in his hands. Pasternak winked at them and gurned disgustingly at the girls.

'Come on then, lass! Do you drop 'em or what?'

Krista was straight back at him, the others laughing heartily.

'Of course we do. We have our reputation to think of.'

'Nederland's liberal tradition is in our hands.'

'And mouths.'

He waggled his eyebrows. 'Swallow or spit?'

First Anke came to sit on his knee, then Krista. Millie started stroking his hair, as all three put on Barbie doll voices.

'Oh, swallow, every time. Which is four or five times a night, in Nijmegen.'

'Yah, that's usual.'

'Five or six, me.'

'I like to go through ten guys on a weekend night . . .'

'Yah. At least. Maybe twelve . . .'

Realising their moralist stance was off target, Tom and Mikey rejoined the group. Matt just smiled throughout. Pasternak leaned towards the girls, reverting to his own voice.

'Tell me though, girls, just for the record – and I do mean just for the record because frankly I AM HUGE and this bears no relevance to me – *does* size matter?'

The girls knelt at his feet and began pretending to take his big shorts down. They'd already been here a week yet they weren't brown. Rather, a suggestion of a light tan seemed to glow from under their skin.

As they strolled back towards the Balcón, reps from competing clubs and bars propositioned them with flyers, vouchers they could exchange for drinks, free bus shuttles to their discothèques. Pasternak's nose for a deal was immediately taken by one special offer.

'Here y'are! Look at this! Club Torro – free entrance before midnight, buy one drink get one free and a bottle of champagne on the house for each group of four! *Now* who wishes they were in Ibiza queuing all night to pay thirty-five quid to get into Privilege?'

The girls winced at each other.

'You know what, guys? Maybe you don't wanna go to this club.'

'Go to Cyclope. It's a lot nearer and *so* much better.'

Pasternak looked hurt. 'But – *free* entry. *Free* drinks. What's the problem?'

'You should ask.'

'Maybe these guys should see for themselves?'

'Sure. Maybe it's all part of the experience, huh?'

Millie chuckled. 'You know what? Let's all go. It'll be fun.'

Pasternak was smelling a rat. 'Now h-h-hang on. What *is* the problem?'

'No, it's cool, Pastie. It just, like – it's not what you might be hoping. *All* those sorts of clubs are free, right? It's no big deal that it's free. I think it would be difficult for them to get people to pay. They're more like, what would you say? They're more sort of open-air compounds than anything you would call a club in England.'

'Cool! Kinda like Space, huh?'

'No. Nothing like.'

'But there's free drink, for goodness sake!'

'The free drink? Murder! It's like this pink, peach

schnapps, yeah? Horrible! Not drinkable! Totally murder! You can't drink it unless you're an animal . . .' Pasternak wiggled his eyebrows again, eliciting more indulgent smiles.

'And the *champagne*! God! It's not even Cava!'

Pasternak looked at each of them individually and apologetically. 'Girls. I think you might be missing the point here. We're four guys from the north of England, on holiday in Spain. We *like* that shit!'

Again the Nijmegen three laughed raucously and clapped their hands.

'You're right! Let's do it!'

'Again.'

Millie sidled up to Pasternak and whispered in his ear, her stud flickering at his lobe. 'You know what Club Torro means, don't you?'

'No, ma'am.'

'Club Bull.'

'Fantastic!'

In the weeks and days leading up to the holiday, Hilary had sworn to herself that none of his stupid little rituals would get to her this time. She was used to it. She'd be able to simply pretend it wasn't happening. This was their sixth Mediterranean holiday together. Add to that two weekend breaks in Paris, one in Amsterdam and one in Antwerp and they'd been away to Europe ten times. On only two of those occasions did Shaun fail to come home transported by the local and national cuisine. When they got back from Crete, for instance, she might as well have been living with an olive. Shaun ate nothing but olives, every day. Fresh Kalamata olives eaten with nothing but bread and a lake of virgin olive oil; lemon-infused olives stuffed with garlic and pimento; mixed olive, onion and lamb kebabs. She ended up having lurid olive nightmares – the filthy stench of those lemon and parsley ones was powerful enough to wake her up gagging one night. And their return from the Dordogne led to a fortnight of strident, cream-based, garlicky sauces as Shaun romped unchecked in the kitchen. His fingers stank of sliced shallots and diced garlic for days after each encounter with the chopping board. Even her Amsterdam duty-free allowance was usurped by his stockpiling lumps of decomposing cheese she knew well would never be eaten.

And the restaurants in those countries! France, in particular, was an episode still too vivid and too painful to recall in any detail. She shuddered at vague recollections of waspish, always male waiters treating them like shit and Shaun grovelling to be liked, effacing himself with his pitiful grasp of French. And he'd *tip* them, after all that! Those bastards had ignored them and served them slop and tittered among themselves as they watched the wretched English couple maul their way through a plateful of dung and Shaun paid them *extra*! God, how they'd fought over that one! That was only last year. Perhaps five years ago she might have admired his deft handling of these international incidents but not now. Not now she knew how to put the bread on the table herself.

She reckoned she could let it all pass her by this time. For over two years now, Hilary had managed a very successful business and enjoyed a very different life. Shaun should no longer irritate her so. Yet her bottom lip already felt worn through from the biting it had suffered since they sat down in this restaurant. She wasn't going to say anything. She *wouldn't* let this spoil things, not on their first night. But, God, she could feel herself losing it! Her husband was a fucking idiot!

She felt disembodied, sitting opposite this man, watching him empty small portions of chopped onion, croutons, shaved cheese and garlic into his soup, nodding his approval. This Expert, loudly and conspicuously relishing this smelly cold soup, knowing the difference and wanting the waiters to know it – who *was* he? A stranger. Some person she hardly knew. Good with his hands and good with his dick – that was all she knew for sure, and couldn't even be certain of the latter any more. She had nothing to compare him with. And she'd forgotten, anyway, it had been so long.

'So you don't mind walking into town while I wait on the car?' She forced herself to make chatter before her antipathy took a real hold.

'I think I shall positively relish the walk. Never know. I might not come back!'

Poor sod. He was trying to be charming. Instead, she found herself despising him more and more. Any warm feelings kindled in the airport and later, in the apartment, were being extinguished with each ostentatious slurp of his soup. Each sprinkle of diced onion made her hate him more, helped her recall more bad things about him. He couldn't even drive. While she was going to be stuck in some poky office filling in forms, proving her identity, *paying*, and waiting an eternity for some clapped-out Seat to be brought before her, that weed would be making the only feeble contribution he could be trusted with. Changing money. He'd go, no doubt, to the first bank he came across, no matter what the rate of exchange on display. He was a big, useless, moron.

'What you going to have for your main?'

'The chicken looked all right –' She couldn't stop herself. '– But you never know, out here.'

He gave his usual half smirk. 'What d'you mean?'

'What I mean is it's more likely to be hen, a skinny boiled hen that'll probably be pink in the middle and, besides, I rather like the look of the sea bass.'

'This isn't Mexico, you know. We're in an EEC member state. The chicken'll be fine, if that's what you fancy.'

What you *fancy*!

'I fancy the sea bass.'

'Good choice. Me too.'

With a conscious effort, she moved her teeth away from her bottom lip and forced a smile. This mood would pass. It was not his fault. She couldn't get to the heart of it and she wasn't going to try. It was bound to be nothing.

'Can you order me another drink? Just a mineral water for now. I want to be able to get up to do my yang before we get going tomorrow.'

Why was she justifying herself like this? *Just* a mineral water. She was going to ask for it without ice, but couldn't face another lecture from him. It'd be simpler to just dump it at the first opportunity.

'*Uno cerveza e uno agua con gas, por favor. Gracias.*'

'Large beer or small please, sir?'

'Er, *grande*. Large. Thanks.'

'So that's one large beer, one fizzy water. OK.'

She smiled inwardly, without joy. If she'd had a

growing sense that these next days were going to be a landmark in her life, then she knew it rudely now.

'How's the gazpacho?'

'Mmm. *Just* superb.'

'Good.'

She sighed quietly and looked out past him at the sea.

They were right. Club Torro was little more than a fenced-off car park, without cars, and with a bar at one end. But the boys loved it at first sight and sound. For a start there was none of the one-upmanship of a nightclub back home, with groups of lads staring at each other and making comments behind their hands whenever someone got up to dance. There was no latent aggression, no fashion snobbery, no self-conscious hanging around at the edge of the dance floor. Most of the punters seemed to plunge straight into the action without even charging themselves with drink, regardless of whatever record was playing. It was a fun-loving, unpretentious, party club where the thrashing hordes greeted George Michael's 'Fastlove' as deliriously as they did Pete Heller's 'Big Love' – and with similarly bad dancing.

Pasternak delighted Anke and Krista by discarding his shirt and roaming the dance floor, tweaking his nipples and rotating his breasts in time to the music. Millie watched from the bar. Only Matt saw her slip out of the side gate, and he reasoned that, if she'd wanted her friends to know she was going, she would have said goodbye. Maybe she had a headache; maybe she was just tired and didn't want to spoil the others' fun.

He lost sight of everyone as the dancing mass grew more riotous. He wasn't much of a one for dancing,

Matt. He could get by if he really had to, but he was much happier watching everyone else. A short girl with a red rose tattooed on her shoulder stood next to him. She looked up and offered a smile. Matt smiled back. He could now see Tom and Mikey paired off with Krista and Anke, kissing lasciviously in the middle of the partying tumult. And there was Pasternak! Talking to the DJ, nodding and grinning, leaning closer to make himself understood. He was giving the DJ his Chas Smash dance. The DJ was shaking his head and shrugging. Matt laughed to himself. The girl next to him laughed, too. Pasternak tried one last time, gesticulating wildly for the benefit of the DJ who shrugged again then suddenly came alive. He tugged Pasternak back and whispered something in his ear. Pasternak beamed and gave him the thumbs-up.

Five minutes later a flushed Pasternak was leading the entire club in a conga around the dance floor, happily flinging themselves from side to side to 'The Return Of The Las Palmas Seven'. Everybody was grinning hugely, everyone cheerfully making a fool of himself. No one was happier than Pasternak, the leader, the party animal. At the very end of the train, Matt felt his balls being squeezed rather too hard by the girl with the tattoo. He thought he might as well. The others were.

Shaun had been aware of various sounds, distant and near, but the combined effect of the heat and the beer and long walk back up all those steps had kept him drowsy. Now, though, it was as though someone had redirected a major sewage pipe straight through one ear and out again through the other. The sound of gushing water was so loud he was terrified a pipe must have burst somewhere in the apartment. He sat up, cocking an ear, straining to divine the source of the sound. It was upstairs. Someone had flushed the loo and the plumbing was routed right through Shaun's cavity wall. Bastards! Had they no consideration?

Clearly not. Moments later an excruciating, distorted screech scraped its eternal path across the ceiling above. It was more painful than any fingernail on any blackboard. He covered his ears, refusing to believe this was happening. Upstairs, they were dragging the table and chairs out on to the verandah, intent, it would seem, on prolonging their night's revels. Maybe they were blithely unaware that anyone had moved in downstairs. Perhaps they had become used to it being empty these past few days. Perhaps they didn't give a shit.

He coughed a couple of times, just to make sure they knew they'd woken someone up. He should really go up there and ask them just to keep it down a little – but that was how fights started. And if these guys were really drunk then there'd be no reasoning with them anyway. Selfish bastards! He'd never *dream* of inflicting that on near neighbours. Never.

And God, it was hot! Now he was fully awake and sober again he could fully feel the intense heat of the night. There was no air to breathe, just the greasy dark heat, heavy and dense. The sweat ran off his arms and legs, making ox-bow lakes behind his knees and in the salty creases of his elbows. Hilary, fastidiously alive to the threat of biting insects, had begged him to keep the windows closed then doused herself in potent Kov mosquito repellent. He might have defied her now and thrown open every portal, but it would have been futile. There wasn't a breath out there.

He could actually hear the conversation above him. They were indulging in what Shaun had come to understand as 'chatting up'. They made asinine remarks about the food, the currency, the Spanish people, and the girls seemed to lap it up. They had put-on London accents, underscored with a hint of yokel. Bracknell or somewhere – real squaddie, estuary boneheads.

'What I wanna know is – how come you get so many facking pesetas to the pound? Eh? I mean, I don't want facking free hundred facking pesetas, do I? I don't know where the fack I am with all that shit!'

The girls giggled. Another dull voice chimed in.

'Yeah, right! They should make a new karren-sea, right, just for us. Fack all that pesetas and francs and shit! Just call the whole fackin lot shits. One shit equals one quid, innit? Easy!'

The girls laughed again, less enthusiastically. They were probably wondering when someone was going to make a move. They wanted their holiday romances to start. Shaun resented them, and everyone, their right to sex. Even the basest specimens were getting it.

Naked and slippery with perspiration, Shaun went to stand in the doorway, hopeful of any stray gust. He thought of Hilary, fast asleep. Earlier, by the pool, a couple of girls had been showing out, trying to get his attention. They must have been seventeen or eighteen, no older, yet their thighs were dimpled with orange peel and cellulite, their abdomens already bulky from drink or bad diet or childbirth. He'd looked over at Hilary swimming serenely, her boyish figure unblemished by any trauma of adolescence and felt again that

45

longing for her. Maybe he could arouse her while she was asleep.

He went back inside and lay beside her, tracing her spine with the tip of his tongue. She shuddered slightly in her sleep and leaned into him, but he couldn't carry on. It wasn't allowed, and the taste of insect spray on her skin was like weedkiller, anyway. He got up again, the brief draught from the door providing negligible respite from the torpor of the night, and swigged some water to gargle the taste away. He paced the room, cursing those bastards in the flat above, obsessing over how he could get them back. And he was going to get them back, all right. They were coarse, they were loud, they were selfish, they had stupid names. Shaun meant to get them back and get them good.

Alone in the apartment, overheating, naked on top of the bed, fatigued but unable to sleep for the jumble of thoughts in his mind, the salt of Pasternak's trickling tears mingled with the salt of his sweating skin.

She'd drifted in and out of sleep. The noise upstairs woke her again, and she was aware of Shaun padding about. There was a delicious draught as he swished the door open before the muggy pall descended once again. He got back into bed and leaned over her, his elbow agonisingly brushing her nipple. She felt his tongue flicker on her back and tried to relax, tried to encourage him without having to face him or participate. She could imagine his rod just a touch away, rising up to its full strength. She tensed, feeling her wetness, waiting for him to ease it in, push it all the way up inside her. She felt ready, but he stopped and went away. He climbed out of bed again and she heard him go to the refrigerator then spit something into the sink. Hilary lay still, eyes wide open, watching nothing. What was she to do? What, oh what was she to do?

Day Two

Nothing. She was going to do what she'd done for the past year or more which was nothing – do nothing immediately, but be prepared. Be ready for what may come, when it comes. For now, for this, the next episode of this, her latest day, that meant ninety minutes of solitude with her yang. She'd already picked a spot by the pool, on the sun deck facing the mountains where a pale sun would rise in an hour or so.

Shaun was still asleep. Unaccountably cheerful, excited even, she swung out of bed with the poise of a ballerina and tiptoed to the fridge for a reviving slug of water. Even with her toned arms and natural body strength she struggled to manoeuvre the five-litre flagon Shaun had hauled up from the kiosk last night. Daydreaming, turning the plastic bottle cap over and over with her fingers, she watched her husband sleeping. Again she was overcome by that fond near-pity for the man. She took another mouthful, spilling more than she drank, and pushed the bedroom door shut with her foot.

Although the blinds were shut tight and the apartment was in darkness, she could sense the brilliance of the day outside. Pulling the thick drapes now and wrestling with the contrary concertina of the balcony blinds, she was momentarily dazed by the bright white light. The nestle of flats and villas slept on below, but the air temperature was already beginning to stifle. Shielding her eyes from the light, she went out to retrieve her swimsuit from the line.

The giggling had come into his fitful dreams a minute or an hour ago, cajoling him back towards consciousness, but these hands all over him startled him awake. Someone was feeling his bottom and at least one more hand was burrowing underneath him, snagging his balls. Matt jolted up, reflexively turning over to see where he was. Three girls jumped back from the bed. Three pairs of eyes dropped to peruse his tackle and three hands shot to their mouths as they went into a giggling huddle.

'I told you! Innee fuckin' gorgeous?'

'You jammy bitch!'

'Giz a go of him!'

'Fuck off! He's mine – aren't you, Matty?'

'Is he a good shag?'

'Banged the fuckin' arse off me! Three times – didn't you, Matt? Fuckin' 'ell!' She rolled her eyes. 'Never known nothin' like it! He's a fuckin' animal! Wunt let me alone!'

'You fuckin' cow!'

'Go on then, there he is! I doubt he'll turn down a threesome!'

'Foursome, you!'

'If 'e's got any spunk left in him! I fuckin' milked him, didn't I!'

They doubled over, cackling. If Matt had felt so inclined or, on another day, obliged, he might have lain back and frolicked with the eager wenches. Much more powerful, though, was the blue mood starting to envelop him. He looked up at them, just three young girls after a good time, and he felt nothing but sorry. Sorry for them, sorry for himself.

'Look – I'll probably see you tonight, yeah?'

He stood up, covering himself as he groped for his jeans. He patted the pocket and tried to pull an expression of relief.

'The lads'll kill me! I've got the fucking key to the apartment, haven't I? Fuck knows where those poor bastards have slept. They're going to kill me. I'd better be off.'

Hampered only by an obstacle course of hugs, squeezes and a 'proper kiss – tongues an' all' for each of them, Matt made his way down the hill, unsure where he was, feet taking him faster than he wanted to go, succumbing to a dull and shapeless despondency. He knew, of course, exactly what this was all about. He'd had long enough to get used to it and each new liaison only seemed more pointless than the one before.

The *point* was this. He couldn't fall in love. He could have sex, had had sex with countless nameless girls and women, but it never felt as though he was involved. He thrust and humped, they writhed and moaned, but he was barely even there. He was a participant who felt nothing. No matter how he tried or what he tried or with whom, he had never since felt the way he had felt with Amanda. Not just that first, unimaginable, wondrous seduction but all the other times, too, when they stole off into the woods, or the old barn, or he crept up to her room and they held each other, shivering in thrilled terror in case anyone caught them. How he'd loved just to lie there afterwards, endlessly stroking her beautiful hair. He'd tried to make sense of it, sat back and viewed it from all sides but he couldn't, just couldn't understand her, let alone forgive her. He was entombed. There was nobody he could even confide in. Seven years ago, and the only person he'd confessed to was Pasternak. He might as well have confessed to a priest for all the feedback he got. He was on his own.

Pasternak patrolled the flat, head throbbing, eyeballs boiling, recollections slowly, so slowly, returning. Had he really led a conga around that club? Had he walked all the way back, throwing stones at the cars that ignored his outstretched thumb? Had he truly been that surprised that everyone had got off with a girl but him? It was a blessing, in a way. They'd be happy. It'd take the pressure off him. As a first-night result, three out of four was not bad. Not bad at all. The lads'd be well pleased with him – if they ever came back.

He rooted through the pile of holiday cassettes he'd painstakingly compiled – for all of them, the bastards – and found the one he wanted. *Holiday Comp. 5*. He felt stupid, immature, ridiculous for the time he'd given and the gurgling anticipation he'd felt making these tapes. Each track he'd recorded provoked a fantasy of how it would be when they were on holiday. In those fantasies Pasternak would be at the heart of all the fun – wanted, included, possibly even desired. Who could say for sure? The sun was known to have a queer effect on people.

'Little Fluffy Clouds' came on. He sighed and shuffled out on to the balcony. The sea looked exquisite. He could kill half a day with the walk down there, a doss in the sunshine and a bit of a swim. He might lose a bit of weight. He grabbed two fistfuls of blubber from around his midriff and groaned again. 'It's all bloody beer, is this!'

Three out of four of them had pulled on the first night. They could stay here a month and that's exactly how the scoreboard would remain. Next to the name Pasternak, a rotund nought. He was a fat bloke. He'd never find anyone who wanted him.

With each stride Shaun was coming more alive to his surroundings. Just below, to his left, fishermen were arguing outside the market, slapping the backs of their hands into leathery palms. Two of them stood watch over the wood grill on the beach, prodding fresh bream with a sharp stick, opening up the succulent creamy flesh to the smoke of the barbecue. Shaun stopped and inhaled deeply, taking in the goodness of all around him. He watched the liquid sun rise up beyond the Sierra Almijara, its slow reveal warning of the aching heat ahead.

Conscious, now, of how little he had left of the cool early morning, Shaun pressed ahead along the coastal path, past the observatory and up the rough-hewn steps to the town. The banks would open at eight thirty. He wanted to be in and out and back at the apartment for nine. With luck, if the car was delivered on time, they could be up in the hills before the sun began to sting. If all went deliciously well, they'd be sitting in the shade of an ancient orange tree by ten o'clock, breathing in its perfume, eating doughy bread rolls, still warm from the oven, dribbling hot butter all over their hands as they sipped the local espresso. He licked his lips as he walked. Paradise.

Matt was mesmerised. Hot, sticky and uncommonly angry from a succession of wrong turns and bad guesses, he had finally spotted a sign and trudged down the dusty approach road to the resort. All he had to do now was cut through the bar and swimming pool compound, take a right, have a shower and he was back on the way to restoration. He felt giddy just anticipating the gush of the shower, washing away the remnants of yesterday.

He cranked open the gate to the pool area and was about to start whistling when he saw her. He was entranced. Ahead of him, standing by the edge of the pool, lost in her thoughts and movements, a woman in a one-piece swimsuit was gliding through a series of floating, sinuous twists and swoops and thrusts. Every part of her anatomy was in motion – wrists, calves, buttocks, fingers – and each elegant sequence seemed to possess a logic, tell a story, almost. Matt sat down, as quietly as he was able, to watch. With total poise and focus, she whiplashed her knee then raised it slowly towards her chin, standing completely still on her other foot, hands held down at an angle from her wrists. She lowered her foot slowly and, seemingly without effort, flicked out her wrists, opened out her arms and kick-danced across the sun deck. It was ballet without music, truly poetry in motion. She bowed minutely, turned and reached for her towel. Only now did he recognise her – the woman from the coach. She hadn't seen him. He'd wanted to applaud but now he felt intrusive. The woman went over to the cold shower at the furthest end of the pool and, as she stepped under its sporadic fits and bursts, Matt retreated to the flat.

He'd rarely seen Pasternak look so pleased. His rosy face positively lit up.

'Matt, me old loves! Hallelujah! Where've you been? Tell me everything! I was resigned to sloping round on me Jack like the sad tosser that I verily be.' Pasternak paused and eyed his mate knowingly. 'D'you shag it?'

'Nah.'

'Why not? Fuck's up with you, man? She was gagging for it!'

'I know.'

'So?'

'Didn't fancy her.'

Pasternak glanced at him and decided to chance his arm. 'Couldn't get it up, more like!'

'That as well.'

'Wait until I tell the others! They'll slaughter you!'

Matt smiled to himself.

'Do us a favour, will you? I wouldn't mind normally, but just while we're on holiday, hey? The last thing I need is those two on my case.'

Pasternak was all tact and sympathy. He put his hand on his friend's shoulder. 'Sure, mate. No problem.' He gave him a little squeeze. 'Happens to us all.'

Matt had to hasten to the shower to suppress his mirth under cover of its splurging jet.

He'd long since learned that when things can go wrong, they go wrong. He should have known it in the bank. He was in there as the doors opened, bidding the cashier '*Hola!*' as he waited at the foreign exchange desk. The meticulous teller with his pristine Lacoste shirt, his neat grey hair and his vulpine eyes didn't so much as look up. Slowly, with all the time in the world, he sat down and began to count and file the various currency denominations. He made a note in minuscule script. Shaun didn't mind watching him work. He had about a fifteen-minute contingency zone, so long as he was back there soon. The bank teller continued working, never once looking up or acknowledging Shaun at all. Other people were coming into the bank, all Spaniards gaily going about their business. Shaun checked to make sure he was in the right queue. He coughed, shifted his weight from one foot to another, affected to gaze out of the window and, finally, began to get irritated. What was with this guy? Did he resent all these loutish, pink-skinned Englishmen with their beer bellies and their crying brats flaunting their disposable income? Fair enough, but a job's a job. Surely he could distinguish between the polite, patient, even cheerful Shaun who was using a local facility and the surly tourists getting fleeced at the cambio kiosk? He decided that the bloke was just having a bad day and elected not to exacerbate it.

Eventually, after an eternity, the guy looked up and barked: '*Si!*'

Shaun jumped to, flashing his most ingratiating smile and began to explain his request in Spanish. The teller cut him short, beckoning him to hand over his passport and his traveller's cheques, and make it snappy, too. Finally making eye contact, but in the manner of an exasperated teacher with a dense pupil, he pointed out in rasping Spanish that Shaun had not countersigned the cheques. He went on the telephone and it was another fifteen minutes before Shaun got him back again. His armpits were dissolving in a swamp of stinging sweat, the soles of his feet starting to slip around in his sandals. The cashier slapped down some notes, a few coins and Shaun's passport and immediately looked beyond him. The grinning, foolish Englishman was just the latest imbecile to step before him and he would not be the last.

It got worse.

'Where on earth have you been?'

'Bank didn't open till nine.'

'Thought it was half eight in Spain?'

'Training day.'

'Trust you!'

He ignored it.

'What's the car like?'

'Invisible.'

'You what?'

'They've cocked it up. Their computer has us down as three days from tomorrow. Which is better, in a way . . .'

'Is it?'

'Well, it i–is . . . It gives us a chance to get a bit of sunshine, then we can cool off in the car for a couple of days, then gradually build up the tan again, nice and steady after that.'

'I'm not really that bothered about a tan.'

'Well *I* am!'

'Well, no problem. Shall we just do our own thing today, then?'

'It looks like it, doesn't it?' She stood there, raking her eyes over him, unable to curb her anger. 'Look at you! Of course you're not bothered about a tan. You've been out in the garden since April doing nothing!'

'Oh, here we go! Go on. Let's cut straight to it!'

'What?'

'You know!'

She rolled her eyes at the ceiling. 'Haven't a *clue* what you're on about!' She knew exactly what he was talking about.

'I'll just do it for you then, shall I? Save us all the bother?' He put on a shrill, unconvincing female nag's voice. 'You're lucky to be going on holiday at all this year! We wouldn't be here if we had to rely on *your* earnings . . .'

'I have *never* said anything like that!'

'You don't need to *say* it!'

'You're paranoid!'

'LEAVE ME ALONE!' He sat down, hanging his head, panting.

She looked at him, pretending to be afraid, knowing she'd won. 'You'd better give me some money.'

He threw the plastic wallet across the room. She examined the bank's receipt. She couldn't let him off. She wanted to twist the knife.

'Only 239? It's 243 at reception. And they only charge 300 commission. So the net result of your two-hour hike into town, Mr User Friendly, is that you've been ripped off. Again. How unexpected.'

She went quietly out of the door, shutting it behind her. Shaun threw himself back on to the sofa. He was a big guy. He'd taken some major knocks over the years and he wasn't one to expect everything to work out fine all the time. But this was wrong. She had done him wrong. He couldn't take it all in, but he was starting to think he'd need a miracle to save him now. Upstairs he heard the sound of someone being sick. That decided it. He knew what he was going to do next.

'Ah, come on, Matt! Don't be gay! What difference does it make if we have a beer now or later?'

'You're welcome, Pastie. I just don't fancy it at the moment. Why don't you pace yourself? After six is fine.'

'After SIX? That's *hours* away. Six o'clock! That's *gay*, that is!'

'I'm not stopping you.'

'Come on! You know I won't drink on my own. Come and have one beer with me.'

'Six o'clock.'

'Six o'clock! What difference does it make if we have a drink now or six o'clock?'

Matt observed his busty pal, already turning pink by the poolside.

'Breasts.'

Shaun held his breath. A group of pensioners made a death dash across the busy dual carriageway. Holding hands, they hunched their shoulders and made faces that said: 'We're going to do a crazy bolt across four fast lanes of traffic now!'

Somehow their inane expressions gave them a shield of invincibility. Cars swerved and missed them, and the old devils disappeared into their hotel unscathed and still holding hands, still pulling saucy faces. Shaun waited at the bend outside the Dumaya until it was safe to cross, amused by the unshakeable faith of the old ones and their utter refusal to understand the dangers of the road.

His good mood continued, and he was actually tittering to himself as his long strides took him back down the hill from the supermarket. He was reassured by the bump and sway of the carrier bags against his shins, evidence of the mischief that lay ahead. He'd bought some things for himself, too. Plump olives, figs, wonky tomatoes the shape of those kitsch ketchup dispensers. He'd bought cornichons too, and some serrano ham, some blue Andaluz cheese and a litre of freshly-squeezed orange juice that had been pressed straight into the bottle as he waited. He'd thrown in a twelve-pack of Cruzcampo to chill in the fridge, and a good-looking white Rioja. He was going to get his work completed efficiently and quickly, then sit out on the balcony, soak up the rays and feast on this local harvest while he listened out for the consternation above.

He let himself into the flat and deposited everything but the jars in the refrigerator. Nervous, now, but only with the same anticipation as he approached his nightly raids back home, he positioned the table underneath their balcony and reached up. With his height and his long arms he was up there with minimal exertion and next to no noise. The patio door was wide open and a symphony of snoring came from within. He checked his watch. Nearly one o'clock. He turned and slowly drew up the washing line, to which was attached one of the carrier bags. As it came within grasping distance Shaun swooped and fished the bag over the plaster balustrade.

Nimbly, he undid the bag from the line, extracted one jar of strawberry jam and another of honey and set about spreading an even layer of each over as many surfaces as he could reach, using the sturdy postcards he'd bought at reception to plaster the goo far and wide. The verandah floor was well covered, as were the windows of the patio door, the table and, with what little remained, a section of the apartment wall. Already, humming insects were beginning to hover. Time to vanish. He placed the guilty postcards in the carrier bag and dropped it down on to his balcony below. Taking care to leave no footprint or any other sign of intrusion, he tied the washing line around his waist and was about to swing back down to his own flat when he spotted her. A travel rep in blue uniform – not Sunflight, thank God – was just standing there on the steps adjacent to the apartment, watching him. Or was she? No – she was talking into a mobile phone.

But she wasn't moving, whatever she was up to. Meanwhile, as Shaun stood there, hordes of mighty ants were starting to march on the EEC jam lake which had been dumped at their borders. He'd never seen ants like them – they were the bold, angry type you only see as an illustration on the side of a pesticide can. And that wasn't all, not by a long way. All manner of droning, buzzing, threatening mini-beasts were starting to circulate, some of them the size of a child's fist, with frenziedly oscillating green wings like thrashing knife blades. He couldn't stay there a moment longer.

Struggling not to catch the rep's eye, and trying to seem as though swinging down from one balcony to another with a rope tied round your midriff was the very essence of normality on a scalding hot afternoon in Spain, Shaun levered himself into position and dropped, landing at the side of his table. Brushing his palms together methodically, he shifted the table to its usual place, rehung the washing line and went indoors to wash his hands. When he came out again, with a beer and a dish of olives, she'd gone.

Matt was dying to talk to her about that spellbinding routine he'd witnessed this morning. He was hypnotised just thinking about it. What could he say, though? How could he approach a woman – not a girl – probably on holiday with her bloke, sunbathing topless while kids were playing all around? He couldn't. He'd tried out every possible intro in his head, but each and every one was a cheesy chat-up or a dud. He'd just have to be patient. A natural opportunity would arise, sooner or later.

Pasternak ploughed down the pool again scattering everyone in his path, trying to breathe himself into a steady rhythm.

'In-ah-ah, out-ah-ah, in-ah-ah, out-ah-ah.'

Matt was right. He was a disgrace to himself. He should be ashamed even to take his top off, never mind flaunting it and making a joke of it. So this was it, then. This was the moment he'd look back on, when he was proudly showing those before-and-after pictures to his disbelieving children. This was the day Pasternak started fighting back.

'In-ah-ah, out-ah-ah.' Fuck! It was hard work, though.

'In-ah-ah, out-ah-ah.' Jesus wept!

'In-ah-ah, out-ah-ah, in-ah-ah, out-ah-ah, thin-ah-ah, fat-ah-ah. AARGH! Fuckit, man! You're a fat bloke! Get out and have a beer!'

And he did. Several.

★

'FACKINELL!'

It took a second or two longer for the true horror to register.

'AAAAGH! AAAAAGH! GRANT! DARREN! WAKE UP, YOU DIRTY KANTS! WE'VE BEEN INVADED! IT'S ... IT'S A FACKIN INFESTA-TION!'

A muffled complaint.

'NO – *YOU* FACK OFF, YOU FILFY PAIR OF KANTS! IT WAS YOU WOT HAD TO HAVE A FACKING FEAST AT FREE O'CLOCK THIS MORNING!'

More muffled conferring, then another voice.

'That ain't us! That's your facking puke they're dining out on, lily-guts!' Shaun raised a bottle of Cruzcampo and toasted himself. Up above, it sounded as though the inmates were perched on chairs like the housekeeper in *Tom & Jerry*, swiping out blindly at any moving creature. Serve them right, the bastards. And the language out of them, too! These chaps were *not* gentlemen!

Hilary sat up and stretched. Media watchdogs could warn and scold as much as they liked, but there was nothing on earth she loved more than the balmy refrain of the sun on her back. Whatever feel-good genes it triggered from within, she was feeling so much better. She'd drifted in and out of a lovely, drowsy reverie all afternoon without thinking much about anything. She'd hardly given Becky and the spa a thought. The sun was seducing her, numbing her mind against cares. She wondered where Shaun was. She'd been snappy with him, perhaps a bit too cutting, but shit! She wouldn't have had such a gorgeously idle day as this, doing nothing by the pool, if she hadn't stood up for herself. He would *never* have let them fritter away a precious day of his precious vacation like this. It all had to be such hard work with him, so much planning and dashing around, getting nowhere. He would never even have let them come to a resort if it had been up to him. A little villa perhaps, or a goatherd's hut. So long as it had no electricity, no facilities and was completely impractical, uncomfortable and inaccessible then he'd be as happy as a daft goose. Poor Shaun. But no guilt, no — he'd been asking for that for ages. No guilt.

She pushed her shades up over her brow, holding back her hair, and looked around her. Straight away she caught the eye of that amazing boy from the coach. He'd been sat a few rows behind and she'd noticed him at once when they'd finally made it on to the coach. He was only a kid, no more than eighteen, but stunning to look at. He reminded her of the sort of fourth- or fifth-generation Africans you only ever see in Liverpool or Cardiff or ports where there's been an influx of cultures for centuries. He had that light brown skin, the merest hint of colour in him, with just a few freckles and so sparse, so spaced out, that it was as though a child had dotted them in with a crayon.

He seemed to exude a natural health and naivety. His broad lips curved slightly upwards, giving him a constant smile. His hair was short, though still irrepressibly curly, but what made him captivating were his eyes. They were bright and lively, but they had a depth and an intensity that she couldn't reconcile. They seemed to reflect the same pleading insight as a trapped animal, beautiful and dignified even in torment, still wanting to be admired but waiting to be understood, too. This was a boy who wanted to be understood, she thought.

She held his strange gaze now and did the only thing she could think of, which was to smile at him. He went a little red and looked away, fiddling with one of his ears self-consciously, but then he chanced another glance at her and smiled back. Hilary was taken aback by the giddy impact of that hopeful, mournful smile. Her stomach vaulted. The boy was getting up. He was coming over! Her groin tingled. Like a big, slow cat, slightly hunched, uncomfortable with his height, he made his way over. She struggled hard to stay composed, feeling an alien tremor shoot through her. It was just . . . silly! She covered her breasts by hunching forward and locking her forearms around her knees. She spoke as he got within distance, finding herself using a neutral-friendly tone she didn't recognise as her own.

'Hello. You were on our flight, weren't you?'

She was pleased at her recovery, the way she'd taken charge immediately without giving anything away.

'I was watching you this morning. I mean . . .' He shook his head at this perceived gaffe, and pulled such an adorable, awkward face, rolling his eyes in embarrassment that she felt like getting up and kissing him. He squatted down so she didn't have to strain against the sun.

'I was on my way back from a club . . .' He was so close that their knees were almost touching.

'Clubs stay open late around here,' she chided, surprising herself again at just how possessive she felt. He wouldn't tune in on that, though. He'd think she was just being a groovy older chick.

'Yeah, well.' He seemed to be in a daydream. Or

maybe he was just thick, struggling to articulate himself. 'I watched your, erm, routine. It was totally amazing. I mean, I just wanted to ask you – what *was* that? Some sort of martial art?'

Her disappointment could not have been more crushing. He wasn't a bit interested in her. Why would he be? Fool, Hilary! Get yourself real! Only yesterday she'd had to lie there listening to women, young and old, whispering about Shaun, gushing over his hair, his chest, his muscles, his dick. Every woman around the pool was in a hot flush over her man, and here she was nurturing the same middle-aged fantasies about a young *boy*. Perhaps it was the sun, or the after-effects of this morning's row, but whatever it was, it was folly. This was a boy crouched in front of her. An eager teenager who wanted to know more about her yang and that was all.

'Mmm. It's called classical yang.'

She was conscious of trying to sound cultured. What did she think she was going to do, anyway? Smuggle him into the apartment while Shaun was asleep? Give him a nudge and say: 'Do us a favour and budge over will you, mate? Just going to knob the toy boy.'

She took a breath, steadying herself. 'It's a form of t'ai chi. T'ai chi chuan, if we're going to get technical.'

He nodded, confused. He was adorable. She felt dreadful, wanting to kiss him so much when nothing could have been more . . . *wrong*.

'Can it, I mean, I suppose it can't be taught, can it? Not like that?'

She felt an overwhelming relief. With a conscious effort, she dragged herself out of her *Jackie* magazine reverie and saw the way ahead and it was wonderful. She was going to help this kid.

'Taught? Of course it can be taught!' she laughed. He looked directly at her mouth and smiled as she laughed. He really did remind her of Man Friday. 'How on earth d'you think the likes of me got into it?'

He shrugged and smiled. 'I mean, could you – shit, no, you're on your holidays. Sorry.'

'What?'

He took a deep breath. 'Would it be OK if I just watched? Just say if that's crap. But I loved what you were doing this morning. If I could just watch, maybe I could pick some of it up?'

She found herself reaching out and taking his hand, smiling right into him. 'I'd *love* to show you.'

He lit up. 'Really?'

'Really. The art is there for the benefit of as many as care to study it.'

He nodded gravely.

'But it is a discipline. You'll have to watch and listen and learn, starting from scratch. It's not easy. And you'll have to be up early.'

'How early?'

'Seven o'clock.' She pointed in the vague direction of the hills, feeling like Grasshopper's bolly-eyed mentor in *Kung Fu*. 'As the sun starts coming up over those mountains.'

He bounced back from the balls of his feet to a standing position. 'I'll set my alarm!'

He smiled his smile as he backed away. Hilary watched him go. She hadn't even asked his name.

'D'you think we'll ever see those two again?'

'They'll have to come back sometime to change their undies.'

'Looks like they've been back already. You'd think they'd leave a note, hey?'

'Mmm.'

'Bastards, hey? Bagging off on the first night.'

'Well. Shuts 'em up, doesn't it?'

'Aren't you arsed?'

'Not really. If it happens and it's right, then great. But I won't feel like I've had a shit holiday if I don't meet anyone.'

'Fuckinell! *I* will! It'll be a disaster! If I don't bag off out here, I'll never bag off!'

'You'll meet someone.'

'Yeah!'

'You will. You've got a great personality!' He grinned at his mate and dodged the cushion he launched at him. 'What a pair of saddos, hey?'

'Speak for yourself.' He looked down, pushed his breasts together and spoke to them. 'What a pair of saddos, hey?'

Matt got to his feet. 'I'm going to have a shower.'

'You're showering a lot, young Matthew.'

'Don't want to let the old BO pile up. I get it bad when it's as hot as this.'

'Stinking heat, hey?'

'Too right.'

'Know what I find about a shower as compared and contrasted with a bath?'

'No, Pastie. What is it that you find?'

'Bad for your balls.' He nodded gravely.

Matt laughed. 'You what?'

'Seriously! Bad for your town halls. Think about it.

You're standing up, so they're dangling anyway, aren't they? But you get sucked into unnecessarily vigorous soaping actions. You treat them with less sensitivity than they might require.'

Matt shook his head. 'You're right, Pastie, mate.' Pasternak nodded with self-satisfaction. 'You *are* a sad case.'

She tried to lose herself in the exuberant courtly ritual of the flamenco, already at one with the confident, concupiscent thrust and flurry of wrists and thighs and strident buttocks. The dance, the act and the story had much in common with her t'ai chi, though coming from a radically different perspective – the one prizing calm self-expression, the other all passionate abandon. For all that the male lead was short and stocky he was fully in control of his sexual charisma, girding his hips and syncopating his bottom to the delight of all the tipsy, snap-happy women in the restaurant. The duelling females, good and bad, shook their girdled busts and stamped their heels, throwing back their jet-black manes as they acted out the rampant drama of the music.

Shaun was oblivious to Hilary's mood. He'd ordered squid and was clearly taken aback when it didn't come in neat battered rings but, rather, a sizeable white valve complete with nodules and tentacles. Undeterred, he proceeded to cut it into neat pieces and surreptitiously flick them out to the skeletal cats by the beach. As she concentrated on the romance of the floor show, she was still aware of Shaun, clapping along, determined to show his appreciation. She'd been so willing to find the good in him when she came back from the pool, but the reality was this gurning buffoon she now beheld. If he so much as shouted '*Olé!*' or '*Bravo!*' she was getting up and walking off. No messing.

When the flamenco ended and the dancers took their applause it was to her great relief that Shaun was not one of those standing up and over-clapping. He poured her a glass of wine and leaned over to take her hand. She looked down at the tablecloth for a second, then tried to jolly herself. No good. It didn't feel natural, this playing at lovers. Her small palm felt leaden in his, but she threw him a smile. He kissed her finger and looked into her eyes.

'No more arguments, hey?'

'No.'

She dearly wished it, like she dearly wished she were twenty again – hopelessly. He kept looking right into her face. She wished he'd stop it.

'We'll have a wonderful day tomorrow. Out in the hills. Just the two of us.'

She nodded. At the table to her right a couple in their fifties sat silent. They had barely exchanged a word, other than to confer about the menu. The flamenco had, seemingly, left them unmoved and they sat there now, perfectly mute, avoiding each other's eyeline. Hilary was desolate. She forced a glance up at Shaun, but continued pushing a breadcrumb around the table with her little finger.

'Where did you decide upon again?'

'Antequera.'

'Sounds nice.'

'You're going to love it.'

No, she thought, I am not. *You're* going to love it. But I'll do my best. I'll do my best.

★

'You're my best mate, you are.'

It was hard enough propping up a drunk, but a drunken Pasternak – Matt didn't think he could keep going much further. Pasternak babbled on, slumped against him but with one arm still automatically hitching a lift. They stumbled and tripped along the dirt track next to the main coastal road, Matt trying to lean all his body weight into Pasternak just to keep him upright.

'You are, though. You're my best friend. I *love* you!'

'You're my best mate, too.'

'But I *love* you!'

'I'm very fond of you.'

Pasternak made a noise that sounded like 'bollocks' then, miraculously, straightened up of his own accord. 'Look at that!'

'What?'

'Isn't it just . . . gorgeous!'

Matt looked all around him. He could make out a road, the vague outline of some shops and apartments and the looming silhouette of the mountain.

'Yeah, it's . . . amazing!'

'How many can you see?'

When Matt turned round, Pasternak was lying on his back staring up at the stars. He gazed up into the clear night sky. He was right. It was awesome.

'Wow! Can you see that one! The shooting star!'

Pasternak started crying. Matt knelt down. 'Hey, buddy? What's up?'

He lurched drunkenly from word to word but was quite distinct. 'Nothing . . . nothing could be better. I'm crying because . . . it's all so beautiful. The world . . . is gorgeous! Life is just . . . so . . . amazing!' He started laughing. 'That's us!'

'What is?'

'Them stars! That's us, that is – looking at them . . .'

Matt said nothing.

'We're nothing, are we? Nothing matters!'

'Come on, bud. Let's get you back to your ken.'

He got his hands under Pasternak's armpits and dragged him to his feet.

'I mean it. None of it matters!'

'I know.'

'I mean – look at you. You went to school in a . . .' He looked as though he was fighting back sick and wafted his hand, as though the action would bring up the elusive word. '. . . an . . .'

'Orphanage. Yeah?'

'And I went to Posh School. And we're both here.'

'Yeah?'

'Futile, isn't it?' ·

Matt grinned at his friend's serious face, a study in enlightenment.

'That's what it is, mate. Futile.'

'WOY HOY!'

They waited for the echo, then cackled dementedly. They'd been at it for hours, up on the balcony above hurling insults at passers-by.

'OY! OO GOES THERE? FRIEND OR FOE?'

'WOP OR DAGO?'

They could hardly get the words out, they were so intoxicated by their own repartee. Then, after an age of puerile chanting, they noticed the echo coming back at them from the gently terraced crescent of the condominium. They were tickled pink by it.

'DAY-GO! DA-A-A-GO! DAGO COME AN' 'E WANT-A YOUR PES-AY-TAH!'

More cackling. Then, to the same tune, they gave full vent to their trenchant wit.

'DAY-GO! DA-A-A-GO! FROGGIES AND DAGOS AND AH-WOPS ARE ALL AROUND US!'

They were nearly dying with laughter. Shaun could hear girls' voices down below, shouting up at them.

'Keep it down, boys!'

'GET UP HERE, YOU SLAG, AND I'LL FACKING KEEP IT UP INSTEAD!'

Dirty laughter from the girls egged him on.

'I'LL KEEP IT UP ALL FACKING NIGHT!'

'Promises, promises!'

'GET UP HERE, YOU SLAG!'

Another voice: 'AND BRING A FACKING MATE, YOU FACKING WHORE!'

'MAKE SURE SHE'S FACKING FILF, AN' ALL!'

'Get ready, boys!'

The oafs roared with laughter, slapped palms and shuffled furniture around. A bottle smashed, to loud cheers. He heard the girls passing by outside his apartment, on their way to their romantic assignation. He felt sick. Everyone was at it. Everyone was getting it. There was no art to it, no craft. You just had to ask – or take. Shaun heard the excitable voices of the girls as they were ushered in upstairs. The lad with the loudest voice boomed out again.

'GELS! JUST ONE QUESTION BEFORE I PORK YOUR BRAINS OUT!'

Dirty laughter. Coy voice in reply, everything about her tone telling him he was on.

'And what's that, like?'

Shaun could not bear to listen. But he had no choice.

'YOU AIN'T FACKING FROGGY BIRDS, ARE YAH?'

'Norr. We're from Chorrley.'

Gales of inane laughter.

'WOY OY! CHORR-LEH!'

Shaun glanced down at Hilary, her face pinched with trouble as she slept. She was so *fine*. He gasped with misery and lay down and tried to blot out the soundtrack from above. He took off his hearing aid and put his pillow over his head, reducing the din to a muffled hilarity, but he could still hear every consonant.

'JUST, FACK! HOW DO I PUT IT! YOU'RE SO FACKING EASY! WE MAY AS WELL OF JUST WHISTLED AND YOU'D OF COME RANNING!'

Shaun heard a slap as one of the girls pretended to be angry. He could almost picture their eager little faces, just waiting for one of these cavemen to drag them off by the arm. They were right. It was easy. It *was* easy, if you wanted it to be. But he didn't want that. He was going to try everything he could to make it right with Hilary. That was all he wanted – to make things good again. If that didn't work, *then* maybe – then he could start owning up to some of the looks and smiles that came his way.

'WE FOUGHT YOU MAST OF BIN FROGGY BIRDS COZ YOU WAS SO FACKING EASY! HEH-HEH-HEH-HEH!'

A sharp slap.

'OY! THAT FACKING WELL HURT, YOU FROGGY FACKING TART!'

Shaun pulled his sheet over his head. He'd rather

suffocate than listen to any more of this. And then it came to him. Froggies, hey? He focused his anger on the day ahead. He knew exactly what he intended to do.

The sounds of lovemaking from upstairs were starting to unsettle her. The girl sounded like she was having a really good time. Hilary, listening acutely, increasingly turned on by those sounds of pleasure, clamped her thighs together, thwarted. Perhaps she should just stir Shaun, try to arouse him. Cautiously, she reached for him, but immediately her fingers curled over his hips she knew it was wrong. She withdrew her hand. It felt exactly the way it had at the restaurant, when he was kissing her fingers. Alien. Awkward. Uncomfortable. She turned on her back and stared up at the ceiling. Fuck. It was over. She and Shaun were through.

Day Three

She hadn't felt this *stupid* since she was about fourteen. Exactly fourteen, actually, waiting outside Preston Guildhall for the guy she'd snogged in the pub the night before, on her birthday, who said he'd take her to see Happy Mondays. The Mondays were on all right. Excitable kids in ludicrous baggy jeans were pushing their way in, but her chaperone never showed up. How bitterly young and gullible and stupid she'd felt as she trudged back to the bus station an hour after the last person had gone inside, angry tears pricking her eyelids. How *stupid*!

And that was what she felt like now. She was angry, not with the boy this time, although it was, with retrospect, boringly obvious that he'd met some slapper last night and had probably only just got to bed. She was annoyed with herself, for being so vulnerable still after all she'd been through. She was cross that a simple no-show by a boy whose name she didn't know had the potential to blow her day apart. And now she had to go and sign up for the car all over again and drive bloody Shaun to some old church up in the middle of nowhere. She couldn't see the day getting any better.

The difficult part had been catching the frogs. Even with the kid's butterfly net he'd borrowed from outside a villa on the other side of the complex, he'd had trouble snaring them at first. The problem was the length of the bamboo cane to which the net was attached; it was just too long to allow any kind of close control. He found himself standing too far back and casting aimless, hopeful swipes over the lilies, optimistically inspecting his catch after each and finding nothing. He didn't want to mutilate a kid's plaything, but then the idea came to him; he could remove the actual net itself from the bamboo and, that way, using it as a hand scoop, have almost total flexion control.

It worked. He quickly perfected a three-act routine of swoop, cover, tip; he'd trap the frog, cover the net with his spare hand then empty out the contents into his bounty bucket. One after another he deposited tiny, bemused frogs, shutting down the snap-on lid before they had a chance to leap out again. He'd perforated the top to let them breathe and inserted sufficient water and foliage for them to survive the short journey back up the steps. Now for the easy bit.

He had misgivings that some of the little frogs might not make it back to the lake, but he was fairly sure they'd be OK. The main threat to their wellbeing would come when the boorish neighbours finally roused themselves and became aware of their little visitors. He'd heard of mice having heart attacks as a result of the terrified shrieks of housewives, and this might be no different. All in all, he considered the end result worthy of the risk.

He got up on to the balcony with ease this time. In the cleaner's maintenance cupboard at the top of the stairs he'd discovered a stepladder along with this excellent bucket. He was up and over the balustrade in a jiffy. Yet again, the patio door was open. He sprinkled biscuit crumbs over all the floors to attract ants, before releasing his plague of frogs. If he wasn't so fascinated by the multitude of haphazard, bouncing, miniature limbs he would surely have been disgusted by the sight. There were dozens of them, maybe sixty or seventy little frogs jumping around the room, a wriggling mass of eddying green bilge, spreading out under the beds, inside shoes and hopping up on to the kitchen surfaces.

Shaun pulled the door tight shut behind him, making sure there was no escape route. He could already hear the little amphibians hurling themselves against the windowpanes. The noise would be sure to wake someone in there soon. If his luck held, he'd hear the results before Hilary got back with the car.

He dismantled the stepladder and took it, and the bucket, back to the cleaner's store. At the top of the stairs he ran straight into the red-haired rep from the day before. She smiled at him. The combination of her pale, gently freckled skin, her rich red lipstick and her perfect white teeth made him stop dead still. Like all guilty parties he tried to look innocent, framing himself instantly as a furtive ne'er-do-well. He shot her the most uneasy grin in all grinning history and hoped desperately she'd take his flagrant blushing for an open-and-shut case of first-day lobster tan.

'Can I ask you what on earth you're up to?' she smiled.

Something about her made him trust her, or to want to tell her. He looked into her playful eyes, that startling turquoise green of the Celts, and he told her. His instinct was not misplaced. She howled with laughter. She had a trace of an Edinburgh accent.

'That's brilliant!' she clapped. 'I wish I'd thought of

that one!' She held out her hand. 'I'm Maggie Maclaren. With Breakaway? I'm up at the pool bar every morning from nine to eleven. Let me know if you've any more sabotage raids on the go. You may need an accomplice.'

She shrunk her neck into her shoulders and laughed again, then she was on her way.

'What are you playing at?'

'What?'

'I've been waiting for you up at reception like a spare part for half an hour!'

'I'm sorry – I thought you were coming back here.'

'What sense does that make? *I* go all the way up to reception and *I* take all the shit from the car hire firm, then *I* come back down again to tell his lordship that his carriage awaits?'

'I'm sorry. I didn't think.'

'No. You didn't, did you?'

It was still so new for her to be dominating him like this that she found it hard to stop herself. She knew where the line was, but she carried on going beyond it. She didn't exactly enjoy the encounter, but it *satisfied* her. She flopped on to the sofa. He'd tidied around, washed the dishes and made the beds.

'You do know that the maid's coming today?'

'I know.'

'So? Why the spring-clean?'

'Just a bit of a tidy-up. Not fair for her to have to walk into a pigsty.'

'Oh, for God's sake! That's what she's *paid* to do!'

Only the uproar from above prevented her going further. It sounded like someone had discovered a

78

mutilated body. The screaming was delirious, other-worldly, out of body. Shaun lowered his head, turned away from her and smirked to himself.

'What the *fuck* was that?'

'Dunno. Probably just one more disappointed camper having a domestic.'

'Sounded like someone woke up with a horse's head in bed with them.'

'Something like that. Come on. We'd better get a move on. Beat the traffic, hey?'

They had to pass the front door of the overrun flat. It was wide open. Startled frogs were hopping randomly outside, some of them starting back down the steps towards the lake, others making short, tentative hops, disorientated by the sunlight. Huddled together at the top of the steps, unclothed and shaking, were three shaven-headed young men and two wild-eyed girls. The only thing that could have enhanced Shaun's wicked enjoyment of the spectacle would have been the knowledge that Darren, the big guy, had only a few minutes earlier been snoring lustily, mouth wide open, when a smothering, choking sensation invaded his sweet dreams. He awoke to find a small frog in his mouth. It would take him some time to recover from the shock.

'Morning!' bid Shaun to the traumatised group, as though he were accustomed to saluting naked groups of deranged folk. He felt good. He felt fine.

But not for long.

'Do you have to drive so aggressively?'

'Said the man who can't drive!'

She was going to say 'loser', but couldn't quite bring herself to do it.

'I'm not criticising you. Don't take it the wrong way . . .'

'Sounds like a pretty critical piece of non–criticism to me.'

'No. I'm just saying . . .'

'Well, please don't *just say* while I'm driving.'

'. . . You know, part of the joy of a holiday is discovering hidden places, opening your eyes to new things. You're just charging past them. You're missing it all.'

'Look. We're going to this old place, aren't we?'

'Antequera. Yes.'

'And we want to see something of this old place?'

He tried to sound amused. 'Well, obviously . . .'

'Well, just shut up and let me get us there. The way some of these bloody erection heads drive, it's going to be dark by the time we get there.'

'They're just farmers. Old country boys. They live life at a different pace.'

'But look at this bastard in front! Why's his back so straight?'

She took her hands off the wheel to grab thin air in frustration. Shaun thought better of answering her back.

'It's written all over him! Straight back, stupid, erect head, stick to the speed limit, obey the rules! Fucking stupid fucking erection head!'

She beeped and flashed at the creeping pick-up truck to move over and accelerated into a scrap of space that barely existed. Shaun put his head in his hands and looked up again only when he knew he was still alive. She turned to him in disgust.

'Oh, stop it, for God's sake! If you could drive yourself you'd know there was no danger! None at all!'

'It's just – you're killing time to save time. It doesn't make sense. Not when you're on holiday.'

'Look, Mr Hippie Dipshit! Drivers like him cause all the accidents! They *invite* accidents! I had to get past him. Right?'

Shaun nodded. They had left Torre del Mar behind and were now making the descent towards Malaga before forking off on to the N331, tracking the Guadalmedina River through the mountains and over to Antequera. This stretch of road was laid with a humming road surface. Shaun well remembered 'humming tar' from tortuous day trips in the seventies. The Ministry of Transport, in an initiative to combat speeding motorists on the motorways, experimented on certain notorious routes with a speed-reactive road surface. The heat of racing tyres above a certain temperature would set off a reaction in the tarmac. Fundamentally, drivers would be warned that they were breaking the speed limit by an unpleasant droning which would increase in volume, rather like a boiling kettle. The sole impact that humming tarmac had upon the highways and byways of the UK was to stimulate ever more brazen outbreaks of speeding as hyperventilating children implored their parents to go faster and faster. He could remember going to Cornwall in the family's Ford Escort Brake – never a hot rod by any standards.

'Come on, Dad! Faster! I can't hear the humming tar yet!'

He smiled at the recollection. The government must have shifted several hundred thousand tons of singing road surface on to an unsuspecting Spain pronto, after the failure of the experiment. He found himself playing out the scene, imaging Arthur Lowe and John Le Mesurier as the civil servants.

'Ditch the screaming tar, Carruthers!'

'What, sir? All of it?'

'Dump the lot!'

'Where, sir?'

'Good point. Does anyone still think we're a nation of engineers and inventors?'

'Hmm. Spain, sir?'

'Excellent. Get on to it.'

They climbed higher and deeper into the spectacular wilderness. Nothing on the coastal strip could have prepared him for this. The mountains were terrifying. Not even in Crete had he encountered so staggering a massif, its remotest peaks snow-capped, even at this time of year. But the surprise to Shaun, the soaring, heart-swelling gift, came with the verdancy up here. Endless pines rode the gnarled backs of the sierras, right down to the rocky banks of the twisting river below. And on the high plains to his left, hunch-backed trees grew back on themselves, their progress blown sideways by a remorse-less mistral. He was drinking it in, wanting Hilary to share in his rapture.

'Look at that!'

'Yes.'

'Isn't that the most fantastic thing you've ever seen?'

'Mmm.'

He opened the window as wide as it would go and stuck his head out, wanting to feel the spirit of the wild terrain blow through him.

'God, it's gorgeous! Can we stop? Shall we have the picnic here?'

'It's not exactly picnic territory, is it?'

He looked around him. 'Well, granted, I see no Ronseal-treated redwood tables with bolt-on benches. But just *look* at this place! It's Eden!'

She sighed. 'I'll have to find somewhere safe to pull up.'

'Sure.'

She drove on. 'I'll have to get us up this hill. Maybe there'll be somewhere on the other side?'

'Well – whatever. But I mean, it'd be best if we could actually find somewhere while we're still up here, up in the clouds. While we've still got this scenery and this view. What a backdrop, hey?'

She kept her eyes on the road. He knew she wasn't going to find anywhere suitable, but he didn't mind so much. Just living through all this was enough for him and he still had the churches of Antequera to come. Things couldn't get any better.

Pasternak was in his element again, taking charge, making the girls laugh. They'd spent the best part of the morning on the beach, burying him, soaking him with buckets of sea water, trying to encourage the boys to make a human pyramid – with Pasternak on top. With the sun now approaching its most destructive passage, Anke was in favour of a long lunch under the shade of the beach bar's olive and lime trees.

'No need for that, An. Just lie behind me!'

She pushed him affectionately. 'You shouldn't make fun of yourself always!'

'But I *am* fun! *Life* is fun!'

He spotted the inflatable banana boat coming back to shore, its whooping passengers getting ready for the routine ducking that ended every trip.

'Cut you a deal,' said Pasternak. 'We all go on the banana boat, then I pay for lunch!'

The girls were in uproar.

'Noooo! No way, big guy! No way!'

'Why not? I'm loaded! They don't call me Plastic Man for nothing, you know! What good is it to me in the bank?'

Mikey interjected. 'Er, slight departure from your usual script, Pastie. What happened to "I might look rich on paper but in cash terms I'm utterly worthless"?'

'Yeah, well – that's to keep chancers like you off my back. These ladies are different. They're worth it.'

Anke was still holding her hands up, smiling in protest. 'Thanks, Pastie. But you're chewing the wrong end of the hotdog.'

'What?'

'We'll be happy to take lunch off you. But no way are we going out on that thing!'

'That thing' was a six-metre-long galvanised rubber banana, inflated, with plastic handles at metre intervals. The challenge was to stay upright as the banana was towed at hair-raising speed around the bay while the girls screamed and the boys looked nonchalant.

'Ah, come on!' By the simple gravitational force of taking her by the wrist and leaning backwards, Pasternak pulled Anke up to her feet. 'It'll be a hoot!'

They walked down to the water's edge, Anke and Krista still laughing in protest. Millie stayed under the parasol watching. Matt called back to her, jerking his head for her to join them, but she smiled resolutely and wagged her finger 'no'. He shrugged, winked at her and jogged to catch up with the others.

The attraction was run by three East Enders. Helping flirtatious girls out of the water were two well-made boys in their twenties, tattooed and so well used to their successful formula that they looked nobody in the eye as they ran through their patter. They took care of the physical process while their father, a silver-haired old rake with a prodigious belly supported by two pipe-thin, spindly legs, handled the money. His sons strapped on life jackets while Dad called out for custom.

'Come on, girls and boys, only a mil for the ride of your lives. One thousand of our Spanish pesos. That's about three quid, to you.'

Pasternak approached him, proffering a five-thousand note. 'Six of us for five mil, mate?'

'On yer bike.'

'Can't blame a chap for trying, hey? There you go. One more makes six thou. Cheers, matey.'

He herded them down towards the banana, the chunky pebbles slowing the progress of their bare feet. One of the brothers looked Pasternak over casually as he approached and held out the flat of his palm.

'Sorry, mate.'

'What?'

'No chance.'

'*What?*'

'You don't want me to spell it out to you, do you?'

He nodded his head at Pasternak's impressive red tummy and held up a compact life jacket. He shrugged an apologetic 'see what I mean?'

'But I've paid!'

'Me old man'll see you right.'

'But . . . I can swim! I don't need one of those!'

He tried a more placatory voice. 'Sorry, kid. Everyone has to wear one, yeah?'

Pasternak nodded forlornly and turned to go back. Matt and Anke went after him.

'Come on. No matter. We'll all go for lunch.'

'No,' sulked Pasternak. Then, remembering who he was, he summoned up a jolly genie from within. 'Hey, no! It's nothing! You lot go on the ride, hey? It only takes ten minutes!'

'Are you sure?'

'*Yeeeeah*! Course I am! I'll go and sit with Mill. We can talk about diet failures.'

Anke gave his shoulder a little squeeze. 'You crazy idiot! See you soon, yeah?'

He watched them go. The young ones. The ones who had it all. Then he turned and went to join Millie.

'Changed your mind?'

'Well, sort of. Someone changed it for me.'

'Too bad. Still – I'm glad I have you alone for a few minutes.'

Pasternak felt a sudden dread panic taking over him. Something about the way she said 'I have you' made him feel trapped, exposed, defenceless. If he wasn't physically shaking then it felt as though he was. Millie came closer to him.

'I just – I mean, it's not so much fun for me now that the other two are kind of living with your friends. They're all so nice, and they include me, but – I don't want to get in their way. It's such a bloody bummer!' She fixed her soft brown eyes on him. He was cornered. 'So I just hoped maybe you and me could have dinner tonight?'

His heart vaulted, with his stomach rising to meet it halfway. He was overcome with a thrilling, sick, nervous excitement and, looming powerfully just beyond it, a choking black fear. Shit! Shit! Why could he not make himself, force himself – just DO it!

'What about Matt?'

She inclined her head slightly, sifting sand through her palm. 'Sure.' She sounded hesitant. 'He could come too.' She looked up and gave the end of his nose a little scratch. 'But I prefer for just us.'

He tried to give an encouraging smile. He tried to show that he understood *exactly* where she was coming from and that, believe me, baby, he was coming, engine racing, from just the same 'hood. He hoped he was coming across as cool and worldly, but he could feel the apprehension in him. The others were making their way back up the pebble beach, laughing about their adventure. As they reached the scalding gravelly sand they started stiffening their legs and leaped towards the shelter of their towels, cheeks sucked in comically – as though that would cool the sand under their feet.

Millie whispered in his ear: 'It's up to you, honey. Matt's welcome. You decide. With or without him, I'll meet you at the cliff bar at eight, yeah?'

'Sure. Can't wait.'

Can't wait for the toilet more like, he thought, holding on to his churning bowels.

The ride down to Antequera stunned Shaun into humble silence. The road followed a gorge through mountainous forests, making him ache to be out there, climbing up and up and looking down. He'd do it one day. Maybe tomorrow. But just as it seemed his heart could not withstand more romance from that boundless panorama, the ranks of spruce started to thin out and the route seemed to dip into gentle descent. As the road cut its slow arc down through the foothills, silent rocks and boulders gave way to burnt clay embankments and sweeps of gorse and brush. But the idle bend of the road gave no warning of the sudden drop from the clouds at its last turn. The last of the spruce clung to rogue red outcrops as the road doubled back on itself and paused and plunged back down to earth. Below, a never-ending green plain spread out to meet the slovenly melt of the *rio* beyond. And at the shimmering, frazzled edges of the sky, just visible in the haze of a white hot noon, glinted the distant escarpment of Antequera. Shaun couldn't speak. It really was too much to take in.

'It smells of blue cheese!'

She was right. Meandering up through the warren of alleys behind the fortress of the Plaza del Carmen, the cloying odour showed no sign of abating. If anything, it was getting stronger, matching the intensity of the midday heat.

'Jesus!'

She made a face. He'd been hoping fervently that only he had noticed the whiff, wanting nothing to threaten Hilary's enjoyment. No. That wasn't it. He knew from the off that she was going to suffer today in silence and he didn't want to hand her ammunition so soon after their arrival. That was more like it. He didn't want her to have reason to hate the place. He stopped, exasperated, already exhausted and sticky.

'Look, I'm sorry. I shouldn't be dragging you around all these churches. I promise you – I won't keep us here all day. But I like this sort of stuff.' He fixed his eyes on her and lowered his voice. 'I like it.'

She dropped her head. 'Sorry.'

He took her arm and tried to smile at her. 'No. Don't be. You're right. It stinks. It's a stinky old town.'

She kept her head down. He looked around, desperate for compromise.

'Why don't you just spend an hour pootling round the leather quarter?'

She looked flummoxed.

'Remember I told you? This place is renowned for leather goods. Might pick up a bargain for your mum. Might be able to find her a nice leather tuffet!'

She laughed. 'A pouffe, don't you mean? Get it right!'

'A genuine Spanish pouffe! God, she'd love it!'

'And who's going to carry it?'

His hair had gone a lighter shade of golden in the sun. He scraped a swathe behind his ear, making his rolled-back eyeballs seem to stare more intently.

'You find it, I'll carry it!'

She looked down at her feet again, uneasy. He was so eager to please her.

'Done. How long have I got?'

'How long d'you want?'

'Tell you what. That café we passed in the square. Bar del Carmen, Café del Carmen, whatever. Shall we meet there at, what? Two o'clock?'

'Two o'clock.'

He leaned over to kiss her. She gave him her cheek and forced a weak smile.

'Sure you're going to be OK?'

'I'm fine.'

'Two o'clock, then.'

He turned and headed back past the ice-cream kiosk and followed a scuttling group of white-garbed Sisters of Mercy and their diminutive priest down the narrow Cintra de los Rojas. He was in luck. It was only as the little side street filtered out into the tiny garden of Plaza de las Descalzas that he became aware of the restoration work and even then only gradually. Overshadowing the gardens, lending merciful cover from the towering sun, stood the ancient terracotta basilica of San Juan. Dotted around the gardens in twos and threes, on benches and sitting on the grass, students and young mothers enjoyed the shade, munching *bocadillos* or slurping at ice lollies. Shaun spotted the wheelbarrows first, then, slumped against the front wall of the church, four or five workmen in overalls dozing and chatting.

He stopped a passing nun, excused himself and enquired, mainly through hand gestures, whether it would be permitted for him to go inside. When she finally understood what he was asking, her round face burst into smiles and she escorted him to the door as if to bestow the Lord's personal sanction. Inside, he crossed himself and stood silently at the back of the vast church, slowly imbibing the frescos, the gilt, the intricate mosaics and, especially, the ornate sculptures and stonecraft. He spotted the area the men were working on straight away. An entire wall of stucco rendering was buckling and starting to come away, raddled by damp and poverty and neglect. The area had been isolated for labourers patiently to strip away the rotten plaster before craftsmen could move in to restore the wall to pristine condition. Shaun's fingers were twitching, wishing he could be on the team, helping this grand old edifice to breathe again. If ever work could give satisfaction it would have to be a job like this – immense, daunting but with the right people and the proper, painstaking procedure it was perfectly attainable. They could help that building live for another thousand years. He sat in a pew of hard, polished wood towards the west side of the church, just to be there for a while.

Hilary was expiring in the dusty heat of the town. Crowds were starting to disperse in deference to the might of the midday fireball and soon only she and the stooped hags, scurrying for cover in their headscarves, were left on the streets. The sun had a sharpness here inland, a bleached-white intensity that she'd never experienced anywhere else. It was a killing heat. A thin man with a spastic leg enclosed in a built-up, protective boot touched his hat to her as she passed. Head down, and sticking to the strips and ribbons of shadow afforded by the side streets, she pressed on, determined to rendezvous with Shaun with something to show for her trouble.

But it was exhausting. Every step brought trickling slicks of perspiration, gluing her lycra vest to her torso. And the town, the place! Why was she here, doing this? It was a farce! That Shaun had persuaded her to drive to this rancid slum was too cruel to be funny. She ducked to avoid the overhanging cables and sidestepped a starved, mangy cat. Ahead was a long, dirty road leading nowhere, as far as she could see. Yet if she turned back, it was a minimum fifteen-minute walk back along the same route, getting hotter and crosser and more fatigued. There was not a sign of life now, anywhere.

The chances of getting a taxi, a donkey even, back into the ancient quarter of town were nil. Shaun!

How she wished that she could share in some way this love of his, this obsession with . . . what? With things that had been here a long, long time – that was what. He liked old things. He *was* an old thing. At least, if she loved churches like he did, she could be indoors, away from the sun's torment. But she felt no such empathy. She liked new things, clean things. She liked now – except she wasn't enjoying this present moment one little bit. She turned back down the Calle Diego Ponce and tried to regulate a cool pace back up to the café.

Outside, the sun had penetrated even the long shadows of the Descalzas garden. It was deserted now, except for the workmen, who were in classic repose, asleep under wide-brimmed hats. He looked at the photocopied street plan he'd picked up from the foyer, with every site of religious and cultural merit marked with a crucifix or the letter A. There were forty-nine. He'd love to see them all one day, but for now he was sated. He had his place in a society of fine individuals who understood the tradition and the miracle of stonecraft.

He made his way back up de los Rojas, little remembering it being so steep. He stopped at the top, panting. Toldos Sierras, the little refreshment kiosk, was still open. Only as he bore down on it, his tongue stuck to his palate with thirst, did he spot the unfortunate owner, his malformed hand hanging over the side of the booth. He was standing on an upturned crate and had really been dealt a bad set. His head was large. It would have looked big anyway, as he measured no more than a metre from toe to scalp, but even given such illusions of scale the poor guy had a gigantic head. He hid part of his extensive skull under an FC Osasuna baseball cap, from which protruded a pair of unwieldly spectacles. He was cross-eyed. Three disproportionate, long fingers formed the flap of hand he used to conduct his business. If miracles were to be had in this religious township, they'd eluded the ice-cream seller.

Shaun hesitated for the merest split moment before making his way over to him. He asked for still mineral water and pointed to a lemonade ice lolly on the chart. The guy indicated for Shaun to place his money on the ledge. He scooped it into his cash bag, fished out change adroitly and flashed him a gummy grin, showing the few brown teeth left in his head. Shaun smiled back with his mouth shut and went to wait for Hilary.

He was early and, spying more nuns in pure white habits heading purposefully along the alleyway at the far end of the plaza, he followed at leisurely pace. He was glad he did so. The small street led to the Iglesia del Carmen and its convent next door. Both buildings overhung a ravine of several hundred feet. The clank of the lone church bell only accentuated the silence that followed. Shaun could hear his own footsteps as he crunched across the gravel forecourt, stopping to sit astride the short stone wall. Below him, clusters of small houses and a dirt road. Beyond that, the gorge and the forest and silence. All he could hear now was the distant hum of the telephone cables.

Getting up on top of the little wall and standing on his toes he could see the Iglesia San Juan and beyond to the green plains on the other side of town. It occurred to him that San Juan must be the highest vantage point in Antequera. He checked his watch. He still had time. There was no way she'd let him off again after lunch.

He hopped off the wall and jogged up ever narrower alleys, always promising to bring him out at the church, always introducing him to another tributary alleyway. The sun was so high and so scintillating that it threw darting shapes, fleeting suggestions of motion up ahead of him. He felt as though he was being watched, as though somebody was just ahead of him, just around the corner, diving out of sight as he turned into view.

Breathless, shirt soaked through and increasingly irritated by the untenable illusion of the church that stayed as near and as far away no matter which path he took, Shaun had a breakthrough. Of course! He'd climb the old ramparts. That was the only way up. It looked easy. Crumbling mortar provided natural footholds, and the wall was no more than ten metres high. Sandals were not the ideal footwear for shinning up an old citadel, but he knew he could make it.

He made it. When he got up there, the church still sat above him, even further out of reach than ever. But the view from the top of the old town walls was astounding. He could see for miles. And what he could see was perfect stillness. Not even a bird flew by to disturb the balmy settle. If anybody or anything was moving down there, they were so slow as to be invisible. He would love to have stayed, to sit there for hours. Reluctantly, but pleased he'd had a taste, he slid back down the wall, scraping his hands and knees this time.

'Please, Matt. Just until I've broken the ice?'

'I don't mind. But I don't see the point. Won't it make you look daft if I come along?'

'No! I'm only thinking of her, really. So it doesn't look like an out-and-*date*, you know? She might get the wrong idea.'

'That *is* the idea, isn't it?'

'*Yes!* But I don't want it to *look* as though that's the idea.'

Matt sighed and shrugged his assent. 'Whatever.'

'Thanks, matey. You're a pal.'

'Can't we just pay for the drinks and get off?'

'It'll come. Trust me.'

'You said that half an hour ago. How long does it take to make a salad, for goodness' sake?'

'They're very proud in these old communities. If he's caught short on something – say he's out of olives or he hasn't got the right tomatoes – he'll nip out to the market and stock up. I bet you.'

'How quaint. Will you pour me another glass of wine?'

'Are you going to be OK driving?'

She shot him a warning look. He poured.

'I can't believe this heat!' she groaned. She drained her glass again. Shaun offered the bottle of mountain spring, droplets running down its sides now.

'No thanks. At least the wine is numbing me to all this.'

It was doing more than that. She was floating, not drunk but detached, removed from the scenario. All that brought her back to reality was the occasional stab of thirst, which she doused with more Rioja. The tormenting sun blazed directly above them, scornful of the pitiful succour offered by the café's parasols. She felt dizzy and slightly threatened.

'Jesus! I *will* have some of that water!'

She sat right back in her chair, trying to form an impression of her surroundings but only managing snatches, snapshots. Opposite her a grand palm stood erect, its fronds tied right back with grass-woven covers to protect it from the ravages of high summer. Behind it were the battered walls of the old town. To the right, the kiosk, now closed. To the left, a shuttered grocery, crates of peaches and limes still stacked up outside. Leading off the plaza at each corner was a dry, silent street or alleyway. It should have seemed idyllic to her, but it throbbed in and out of focus. A persistent tone, a ringing she could neither place nor master drilled at her inner ear.

'What is this place?' she muttered.

'Wonderful, isn't it? Glad you came now?'

She said nothing. He took it as awestruck concurrence.

'This is what Spain's all about. Forget your crowded beaches and your cod flamenco! This is it, hey?'

She drained her wine glass, recoiling slightly from its instant kill. He read from his information sheet.

'Do you know that there have been more sightings of the Virgin Mary in this town than anywhere else in the world? This is where they think the reincarnation is going to take place. That's why there's so many stunning churches and convents in one small place. Everyone's just waiting for a miracle.'

'Fascinating.'

He smiled right at her. 'All you can do is be ready, I suppose.'

She concentrated on his mouth moving as he spoke. He looked ridiculous. His hearing aid seemed outlandish, disproportionate to his small, hairy ear.

'You stupid old man!'

'What?'

'You're just a silly, stupid old man, aren't you?'

'Are you pissed?'

'Pissed off. With you.'

He looked so crushed that she had no option but to continue. She had to carry on.

'Old churches! You fucking old fart!'

She saw tears water those mad, bulging eyeballs, the eyeballs she couldn't stand having to look at now. She wanted to rip his earpiece out, just to do it, to have done that to him. The hoary old proprietor chose this moment to proudly bring out their salads and it was that moment that convinced Hilary she had to get away from Shaun.

The salads were, admittedly, like none she'd ever seen, teeming with leaves and peppers and gherkins and a tumult of shaved cheese, pimentos, tiny boiled eggs, luscious tomatoes and a basket of bread still stiffening from the oven. And Shaun, heartbroken, choking back tears of rage and hurt and injustice, did what? He hid his feelings. For the benefit of the old café papa, so as not to let him think his feast would be wasted and to make him believe that this young couple would go away only with the most cherished memories of him and his town, Shaun stood up and applauded the old man as he carried their tray to the table. How could he do that? Cut to the core, how could he find it within himself to continue this play in which they, the wide-eyed lovers, would delight in the abundant hospitality of this tiny, old-town community? He was unreal.

The old boy took her hand and kissed it and bestowed a smile upon her that made assumptions about being young and in love. She tried to force a return smile and probably acquitted herself as a blushing English rose. The proprietor clasped his hands together, said something in Spanish, crossed himself and backed inside the café.

Shaun looked down at his plate and started stuffing leaves and eggs into his mouth. His head hovered six inches above his plate. He didn't look up at her. She felt like smashing his face down into his precious salad. The piercing note droned on. Electric cables? It was maddening. The immovable sun beat her brow. She imagined being up there, right up on top of the sun looking down on the earth, watching Shaun in his little seat outside this little café. She felt sick. She stood up and gripped the edge of the table to steady herself, trying to breathe slowly, deeply. Shaun didn't look up. She walked away towards the car. He carried on eating, face down, munching lettuce.

All that was kicking this on now was instinct – it was all animal, no plan. Her mind was numb, locked stiff, unable to filter through the events that had just happened. She was aware that she was driving away from her husband and that she had to continue driving. Her mind throbbed with the protest of the engine, rattling along in absent third gear. She had to press on, push away from him or she would still be sitting there, looking at that fucking earpiece. She could have crushed it to shreds under her heel and spat in his face for making her look at it for all those days and days.

Ten kilometres out of town, starting the climb up the approach road through the National Park and, ultimately, the Malaga road, she pulled over, pricked by doubt. In the shelter of the car with the chill blast of its fan, the ringing in her ears slowly subsided along with that disorientating headspin. Apart from the faint afterburn of the wine, she felt comfortable again. She felt normal. She thought of Shaun, struggling to hitch a ride in the naked drought of the flatlands outside the town. She couldn't just leave him there. Yet she had to. To go back now would merely be to stem a flow that would only burst through again, soon. Without a sincere notion of why, she just knew that she needed to see this through. When she'd booked this break, months ago, she'd had the germ of an idea that her future with Shaun would depend upon these few days away. Now she knew it resolutely, but in a radically different sense than she would have admitted even a few months ago. Even allowing herself to face that bitter reality, she still had no clear plan. She'd just have to see. She pulled back on to the mountain road and had to let herself allow that these were spectacular surroundings.

He laughed to himself again. Content just to be sitting back on this air-conditioned Alsina Graells coach to Malaga, having enjoyed their slow haul through Villanueva de la Concepción and shiftless progress beyond, he wanted to try and get to the heart of Hilary's crisis. He wanted to see it from her point of view – but all he could see were the nuns' shocked faces. He'd devoured his own salad, finished Hilary's, tucked the bottle of water in his knapsack and left money on the table. He knew the old boy would be asleep by now, happy to have served. His mind troubled by Hilary, he ambled down the cobbled slope in the vague direction of where he imagined the bus station would be.

Heading down Avenida Encarnación towards the Plaza San Sebastien, still preoccupied with her, he found himself amid a gaggle of nuns all chattering outside their convent. One by one, as they noticed him and tugged at their neighbours' surplices to indicate him, they started to drop to their knees, some wailing, some smiling in terror, prostrating themselves before him. A young novitiate crawled towards him and kissed his feet tenderly, lavishing his sore ankles and toes with tiny, pecking embraces. Her intention was supplication, not arousal, but Shaun's balls started to tingle. It was a mirage. He was being seduced by ultravixen rave nuns! He tried to stifle a shameful erection with thoughts of blue cheese when the nuns began murmuring: 'Jesu! Jesu Cristo! Spirito Domini!'

What they had seen was a shambolic Englishman with long hair, a scuzzy beard and eyes so blue as to appear sightless. This hapless tourist, as a result of his impetuous ascent of the town walls, was bleeding from the palms of his hands and his knees. It wasn't quite the full set of stigmata, but it was enough to convince the nuns from the Convent of the Incarnation that this was what they'd been waiting for. The Second Coming. Jesus Scanlon, the stonemason, had arrived in their midst, to deliver them. And to ask the way to the bus station.

He smiled sadly. His unhappy wife would have

relished the episode, once. He was going to have to get himself up a mountain and think things right through.

He could kick himself for sleeping in. It was Pasternak's fault. When they'd finally stumbled back to the apartment last night, Pasternak had insisted on sitting out on the balcony looking at the stars and wondering at the endless possibilities of existence. Matt had had to stun him to sleep with brandy.

He'd been hanging around by the pool since three, hoping to see her, wanting to explain to her why he hadn't made it to t'ai chi that morning. The sun was starting to burn itself out. He was about to give up and go and get ready to hold Pasternak's hand on his dinner date, when he saw her coming through the far gate to the pool. She looked bothered. He was sure she must have seen him but waved over, regardless, keen to head off any sort of prolonged charade. She smiled and waved back and came to sit next to him, dangling her feet in the pool.

'Ooh, that's divine! Mmm! The simple things, hey?'

He nodded, waiting for her to continue. She didn't. She stared out over the trees and bushes.

'Sorry about this morning.'

'No need. I was here anyway, remember.'

'I know. But I did really want to get here. Just . . .'

'Don't worry.' She forced a knowing grin. She was eating herself up with curiosity. She couldn't stop herself. 'I hope she was worth it, anyway!'

Matt's face almost throbbed with surprise. 'Oh, no, no – nothing like that. Unfortunately.'

She found herself stirring the water more intently

with her feet. She made a conscious effort to relax. The boy hadn't noticed a thing.

'No, my pal chose last night to get to the bottom of the meaning of life.'

'Did he find what he was looking for?'

'No. He was looking in the sky.'

He turned and looked right into her eyes. 'Are you OK?'

'Yes! Fine . . .' She felt herself slipping away.

'Good. You look like you're a million miles away.'

'Up there in the clouds with your friend, wondering what it's all about.'

'I can save you the trouble.'

She found herself talking in a Maid Marian voice. 'Please do, sire.'

Fuck! Stop flirting! Stop being such a *girl*! He didn't seem to notice. He carried on, head down, frowning slightly.

'Nothing. It's about nothing.'

'Very profound.'

'I don't know. You're definitely OK?'

She watched her toes trace currents in the pool.

'No. I'm not *that* OK, as a matter of fact. But I can't really talk about it. Not until I know what I think. Which I don't, at the moment.'

He shot her a grin. 'Very profound.'

'Don't tease me.'

'Sorry.'

He stood up, stretching, the oblique muscles around his ribs straining with him. He looked down at the sea, talking with his back to her.

'Look. It's none of my business. Talk if you want to,

if not, don't. But, well, erm . . . you might be able to help *me* out.'

'Me?'

'Maybe. Oh, fuck – I don't know! Sorry.'

Even from behind she could sense the mad blush of his neck and ears. She tried to help, adopting a playful tone.

'No, go on! You can't just leave me dangling!'

He turned around, unsure. He spoke falteringly, looking at her gravely. I've been sort of . . . roped into, like, riding shotgun for my friend, right?'

'The existentialist?'

He paused and thought. 'Does that mean Fat Bloke?'

She laughed. 'I believe it does.'

He continued, more relaxed now. 'He's been asked out by this girl, right. She's nice, but I think he's scared. He wants me to come along with him.'

'Aaah! He sounds adorable.'

'He is. Well, like, I mean he's all right, you know? But I reckon I'd be doing him a favour, like, if I blew him out.'

Don't flirt, don't flirt. Don't show any remote hint of intrigue. You can even play it a little bit fierce.

'And where do I come into this master plan?'

If he was puzzled by her aggressive tone, he didn't show it.

'I dunno. I mean – it'd be nice just to go for a walk, hey? Take the cliff walk into town. Have a coffee. Whatever. If I could just sort of look him in the eye and say I was going out with a lady myself . . .'

A *lady*. That made her sound very grown-up. She looked at the boy's handsome, open face, his uneasy brown eyes expecting rejection. Maybe he had no ulterior motive. Maybe he did genuinely just want to befriend her. She couldn't be bothered analysing it and, whatever, she didn't mind either way. What would be, would be.

'Am I going to learn the identity of my chaperone?'

'What?'

'Call me a stickler, but I'd be happier if I knew your name.'

He slapped his palm against his forehead and grinned. 'Doh!'

She laughed with him.

'Sorry! I'm Matt.'

He held out his hand to her, still shaking his head. 'Sorry. I'm such a dickhead.'

'Accepted. Er – shall I tell you my name? Or do you prefer Mrs X?'

He slapped his forehead again, smiling.

'I'm Hilary. I think I *would* like to go for a coffee with you, Matt. Thank you for asking me.'

His eyes danced.

'Great! That's just great! I mean – I promise I won't try anything on, like! Shit! Sorry! You know what I mean . . .'

She shook her head, amused. 'I'd just quit while you're ahead.'

'Definitely. Shall I just meet you down at Ayo's at about eight o'clock?'

'Perfect.'

'Good. I'll go.'

He gave a little bow and was gone. Only then did her thoughts return to Shaun. She knew she wasn't being fair to him. She was being fair to herself, instead.

★

'Don't do this to me, man!'

'I'm doing you a favour!'

'You treacherous bastard!'

'How come?'

'Desertion! You're deserting me in my hour of need.'

'I'm fucking helping you out!'

'You absolute bastard! I'm – I'm cutting you out of my will!'

Matt looked at the irate Pasternak, all scarlet, angry dough and couldn't help loving him. He went across and hugged him. 'It'll be fine, mate. You'll see.'

'Ow! Mind the sunburn, will you?'

Shaun was picking his way around the potholes of the lane down to the resort when the black Suzuki Vitara that had passed a moment ago reappeared next to him. It was Maggie.

'Don't tell me. You've been up to the German resort to adulterate their muesli with amphetamine sulphate?'

She had the roof down, hair loose, sunglasses on. She had that same playful smile, seeming to know it all already. On a whim, just as he'd confessed to her about the frogs this morning, he decided to call her bluff.

'No. I've spent the last four or five hours making my back from Antequera by public transport having been abandoned there by an irate and somewhat unreasonable wife.'

If he'd been looking for it he would have seen a twitch of disappointment, but she recovered straight away. 'What did you do to her? Put jam in her knickers?'

He found himself shuddering with laughter. He threw back his head and guffawed hugely at the preposterous image of Hilary discovering jam in her pants. 'If only you knew how ridiculous that is!'

She was pleased with herself, pleased that she'd made him laugh. She hesitated, watching him compose himself. 'You look like you needed that.'

'Ah, no – it's not so bad. I dragged her off to see churches when she wanted to stay on the beach. I'll just have to go on my own, next time.'

She knew he didn't mean it. She examined his troubled eyes, his flinching expression. She felt an overwhelming sympathy for this big, sad man, and a will to do something nice for him.

He smiled bravely. 'Well. Lovely to talk to you.'

'And you.'

He started off down the hill again. She shouted after him.

'Look! We have a day trip to the Alhambra Palace tomorrow, if you're interested?'

'Really?'

'Yes indeedy!'

He looked away at the winking dapple of weak sunlight on the waves.

'Actually, I'm just being polite. I can think of nothing I'd like less than to sit on a coach full of holidaymakers "doing" Granada.'

She laughed. 'You horrible snob!'

He inclined his head. 'That, madam, I am.'

She howled with laughter. 'You're too right! I was only inviting you along to keep me sane. Ah, well! Leave me to my own devices, eh?'

He smiled and tossed his hair out of his eyes. 'Nice of you to think of me, though.'

'Aye. It was, wasn't it? Good luck with old jammy drawers, anyway.'

She started up the engine again and waved as she skidded away. He watched her go. He hoped old jammy drawers was not back yet. All he wanted now was to sit out on the balcony with a bottle of cold beer and watch the sun go down.

From her spot at the furthest point of the Balcón Europa, the twilight gave the mountains a mystical purple hue. She stood slightly apart from Matt, comfortable with his presence but enjoying the heightened sense of isolation the music evoked. In the middle of the plaza a troupe of pan pipe players lulled the sparse crowd with their disconsolate melodies. Something in the forlorn timbre of the pipes seemed to match the romantic melancholy of her mood. As the maudlin red sun sloped behind the mountain bow, the players eased into the soaring drama of Rodrigo's *Concierto de Aranjuez*. Hilary swallowed hard. The pleading clarity of the flutes told out her own loneliness. She dragged her teeth over her lip to stop her tears, but it was hopeless. Silent, convulsive sobbing racked her slight body. She put the back of her hand to her mouth to try to stop it and, eventually, found herself laughing at the folly of her situation.

Matt placed his hand lightly on the slender curve of her hip. 'Hey! What's up?'

She laughed. 'Really, nothing. It was just the music and the sunset and the mountains – I'm a girl, dammit! Let me cry!'

He smiled that open, inviting smile of his. 'Whatever you say. You sure you're OK?'

'I am, and . . .' She leaned up and pecked him on the cheek. 'Thank you. It's been lovely. I just want to walk for a bit on my own now.'

He stepped back slightly, dismayed. 'Sure.'

She took his hand gently. 'You've been lovely. I'm sorry I haven't been much company. I just need to be on my own for a bit, I think.'

'OK.'

'Well.' She let his hand go. 'I'm sure I'll see you by the pool. Or whatever.'

'Yeah.'

She walked away a few paces and, conscious he was watching her, she turned and waved, then mingled in with the crowd.

The more they drank, the more he relaxed. It was going to be fine. He liked her, she liked him. This could be it. This really could be the one. Pasternak leaned over the table and took her hand.

'So. Millie.'

'Darling Pastie?'

'You're a bit of a porker, aren't you?'

Day Four

He'd heard her come in and she'd kept him awake, tossing and turning in the oily night heat. But he played dead. He'd made his mind up to be out of there at first light, even before Hilary rose to embrace the day. He was going to steal a march on the sun, get himself halfway up the mountain before the humidity had a chance to sap him. Things would look different from up there.

He made a good start, getting up beyond the Roman viaduct at Maro and tracking the river a mile inland without pause. The day was fresh with a sky hung low by a thousand chubby white clouds, waiting for the rising sun to burn them off. But the terrain was becoming more severe with each twist of the parched *rio* as it gouged its path through the rock. He caught his breath as he leaned back against a flat cliff face to plot the route ahead. The river path was getting steeper and, half a mile ahead, would barely be navigable as it passed over the deep ravine. He could break off to the right before the gorge and start his ascent of Mount Navachica the slow way, using the goat trails. The sun had started to announce itself and would be fully flagrant in an hour. He took a hit of water and pressed on.

She felt oddly optimistic. This sensation that things would turn out for the best, somehow, was a novelty. It made her realise how down she had been, generally, for far too long. She was nowhere near an understanding of what was happening to her, but she had an inkling that she should continue to hold out, to see what *would* happen to her, or what she could bring about. The uncertainty was strangely liberating.

She was sorry for savaging Shaun like that yesterday and sorry that he wasn't here now. But she was glad of the space, too. All she knew for sure was that she was going down to the beach to swim and lie around and watch the world go by.

'How've your shits been? If you don't mind me asking.'

Matt was finding his prolonged exposure to Pasternak starting to grate somewhat. He didn't want to go swimming. He wouldn't play volleyball or beach tennis or go on a pedalo. Matt had even suggested hiring a car and going off somewhere, but he didn't seem keen on that, either. Doctor Fun was turning out to be a bit of a bore.

'Mine are just like putty. Must be the sun melting all that crap in your guts, hey? It must blast it down like an ore foundry.'

'Know what? You're a really, really disgusting cunt, you are.'

'Lan-guage!'

They shuffled down the last few steps and made the familiar journey to the mini-market. They did the same thing every day. They looked around the gifts, souvenirs and T-shirts and the dizzying array of vicious orange espadrilles – then Pasternak would buy the *Daily Mirror*, loads of crisps and Coke and they'd go and sit on the beach. Matt was genuinely pleased that Tom and

Mikey had found the Real Thing – they were besotted – but he was restless. He didn't know what, but he wanted more than this from his holiday. Pasternak howled with laughter.

'Fuckinell! Look at that!'

He was riffling through postcards and held up one that read, in groovy, flower-power graphics: *Spain Is Different!* It featured a comely blonde with three breasts. Pasternak brandished it at Matt in delight.

'Quality! Pure quality!'

There was a whole series of them: a computer-generated freak show of midgets with stupendous nipples, waitresses with strident willies and jolly, lactating African ladies. Pasternak couldn't stop staring at that one. He bought the entire collection of six cheeky cards.

'Who are you going to send them to?'

'Me.'

They crossed the road to the beach.

'Pointless asking if you fancy a dip?'

'Futile.'

They sat in silence, Matt sifting sand with a bleached lolly stick.

'So?'

'What?'

'Aren't you going to tell me how it went last night?'

'It was all right.'

'Is that all?'

'Pretty well. What about you?'

'We're not talking about me.'

'We are now.'

Matt drew a swirling pattern in the sand. 'I dunno.'

'Well, if you don't, no one else does, hey?'

'You know what I mean. It was weird. I fancy her, like, but . . . Fuck! It'll sound weird, right?'

Pasternak nodded, inviting him to continue.

'There's something about her. I think I could talk to her, you know?'

Pasternak nodded again. 'So what happened?'

'Ah, fuck knows. She got a bit emotional. I think she's just split up with a guy or something. I dunno. She legged it, basically. Doubt if I'll see her again now.'

Pasternak started laughing.

'What's funny?'

'You! The great stud takes a bird out and she runs off, crying!'

'And that's funny, is it?'

Pasternak's eyes were shining. 'Ooh! Touchy! Sore point, sore point!'

Matt flapped a dismissive hand at him. 'Ah, leave it out, big fella. You don't know what you're talking about.'

But Pasternak's attention was elsewhere.

'Uh-oh!'

'What?'

Down at the fishermen's end of the beach, making their way towards them, were Mikey and Tom and the three girls. Matt's face lit up.

'Ah, good one! My volleyball team!'

Pasternak looked haunted.

'Listen. I'm not in the mood to be jibed by those two today. I think I'll get off.'

'What you on about?'

'Them. The Smugs. If they're not sitting there stroking their birds' hair or holding hands then they're going on at me about . . . exerting myself.'

Matt laughed. 'Nutter!'

Pasternak held out a flat hand decisively. 'No! I am on holiday! I have no wish to exert myself.'

He got up. Matt shielded his eyes against the sun as he looked up at his friend.

'Ah, stay, Pastie! The lads have hardly seen you.'

'Their fault, their loss.'

He picked up his transparent, inadequate mini-market plastic bag and marched off, giving every impression of being in an almighty huff. A minute later the others arrived.

'Was that Pastie wobbling off into the sunset there?'

'Sure was.'

'He looked just like a big strawberry jelly. He was positively shuddering.'

Millie broke in. 'Where is he going?'

Matt shrugged. 'He's been a bit weird all morning. He just sort of stood up. And went.'

She nodded sadly. 'I guess I know what that's about.' She sighed. 'He's such a funny boy. I don't know.' She turned to Matt. 'I don't mean to be, like, a pain in the ass but . . . maybe later, when you feel like it. Will you tell Pastie not to feel embarrassed? I'm fine with him. He'll know what I mean.'

Matt nodded and got to his feet. Millie held his wrist.

'Not now! I didn't mean for you to just run and do it!'

'It's no problem.'

The others joined in.

'Leave it for now, Matt!'

'Honestly! I can be there and back in ten minutes. I'd rather! Otherwise the poor git's going to be sat in the flat on his own, sulking. I should've guessed there was something up with him.'

He gave them a thumbs-up and jogged away to the steps.

He elected to stay where he was, on the plateau. He'd need better equipment than he had now to make a proper attempt on that final stage. Decent boots would have been a good start. From below it was impossible to appreciate the ruggedness of these upper slopes. The goat trail had taken him up at a peaceful gradient, demanding little more than a sustained hike from him. But a rockfall blocked that pathway about halfway up. The last hour had been hard going. He had needed to physically climb, hand over hand, to the ledge where he now sat, enthralled. To go any further would have been foolhardy, and for a view that could scarcely have been any more dramatic than the daunting vista he now presided over. If anything, the clouds still drifting above would impair the view if he went much higher. He sat with his legs dangling over the edge, a mainly sheer drop of a thousand feet, confounded once more by his own insignificance. A renewed feeling of humility came over him. He was nothing and his troubles were nothing. He felt that, if he gave himself up to the elements now, if he trusted himself to the wind, it would bear him safely back down to earth.

He tucked his knees under his chin and reached inside his haversack for the simple lunch he'd prepared. Two boiled eggs, a wrap of salt and pepper, a small chunk of Parmesan and half a stick of bread, which he was going to soften with a drizzle of lemon juice. He ate energetically, chewing quickly and sipping at the now tepid water, all the while trying to absorb as much of the scenery as possible.

A dark shape hovered at the furthest extent of his field of vision. He twisted his head up and backwards to get a true sight of it. It took a moment to compute. Coasting the thermals, floating way, way up on high, swooping and gliding with menacing grace was a bird of such mythical dignity that to see one now, just there, brought tears to his eyes. The eagle soared upwards, partially blocking the sun. Shaun stood up, shielding his eyes, watching the magnificent bird-beast describe its own flamenco with its powerful swoop and span. For a moment it let the wind drag it so close to Shaun that he could look it in the eye – not the avaricious yellow he expected, but a wise and regretful black. He held his breath until he thought his heart would burst and only when he let it out again did he find himself on a rock, high up in the sky, laughing out loud for the sheer joy of it.

He expected Pasternak to be slouching on the sofa or out on the verandah, so it was with an element of surprise that Matt let himself into the flat to find his friend with his back to him, shorts down. He observed his dimpled buttocks quivering with the momentum of the rampant Pasternak, jerking his penis ferociously with one hand while he held up a postcard of a three-breasted woman with the other. Matt backed out of the apartment before he witnessed any more than he had to. Exertion, indeed!

She was going round and round, trying to straighten it out in her mind. She was now reducing the whole thing to a childish list of Good and Bad, and it was mainly coming out in Shaun's favour. So, if he was that good, why did she feel so bad about him?

She wanted to be tough on him. She wanted to show herself how much she'd changed, how she was capable of taking a radical, grown-up stance if the need arose. So whenever she found her mind drifting off to cosy reminiscence she tried to fight it off with practicalities. And that just meant more lists. So she gave in, remembering her first sight of him when he was working on the exterior of the Britannia Hotel. She noticed him then because of his physique, burnt deep brown in that hot summer of '95, and because he was the only one of the workers without tattoos. But when she bumped into him at the station, it was his meekness that struck her. She was amazed that such a big, strong guy – a bricklayer, as far as she was concerned, a building-site bloke – could be so gentle. She was going home for the weekend and she remembered well the way Shaun had come bounding down the steps four at a time, craning to read the information display at the same time. He'd asked her whether she'd noticed if the Chester train had gone. He was so polite that he seemed to be from a different era – she felt she knew what it was like to meet Sir Walter Raleigh. That courtliness was so appealing, back then.

An announcement had come over the public address that all trains were delayed indefinitely – a staple Oxford Road announcement most Friday rush hours. They ended up having coffee in the Corner House and she found herself on a train to Preston two hours later nursing an almighty crush on him and a dinner date for Monday night.

And how wonderful those first weeks and months were. His intuition sought out her inexperience without her having to splutter and fidget and come out with all the usual excuses. He just seemed to know and to understand from the start. He was heavenly, the more so because, by that time, the start of her final year, she was starting to fear that sex could become an issue with her. It was difficult. She'd had lots of boyfriends and she'd made up her mind when she was sixteen that she'd let the next nice boy talk her into it once they'd been going out for a couple of weeks – a month, maybe. But it just hadn't happened. And then, at Manchester University, she was afraid of the word going round. There simply didn't appear to be that many eighteen-year-old boys who could be entrusted with relieving Hilary of her virginity. If she chose the wrong guy or if she froze or if something else went wrong then it would be all round the place. Hilary Best is a fridge. Hilary hasn't done it yet. She'd rather not risk it. So she gleaned what she could from *Marie Claire*, stayed pretty quiet during her girlfriends' lurid sexual post-mortems and went home at weekends, alluding to some wonderful, if madly jealous boyfriend.

So he was a godsend, Shaun. He was romantic, sensitive and had the looks of a Spartan warrior. They dated for about six weeks without sexual intercourse being mentioned, though Hilary had twice tried to satisfy him manually, in her car. She was certain the act was supposed to end with ejaculation, but on both occasions he'd placed his big hand on her oscillating wrist, thanked her and zipped himself up. He later confessed to harbouring feelings of jealousy towards the car's gearstick when she wrenched it from fourth down to second, as she handled it with so much more sensitivity than she'd afforded his dick.

They *had* talked vaguely about going away to Paris and she understood, vaguely, that this would be the scene of her deflowering. But she'd reckoned without the tact and sheer sympathy of her lover. During the same confession about her masturbatory technique, he also admitted his fears about making love to her in a Paris hotel. He felt that the setting, the theatre, the almost ritualistic element of taking her maidenhead would most likely make her sick with worry. Which was why he'd taken her by surprise during a routine groping session in the back of the car and fucked her silly. Really. She felt as though Duraglit would not remove the big, stupid smile that stayed on her face for three days afterwards. She was a woman.

And she loved sex! She wanted to do it all the time, all over the place, in as many new positions as possible. In one of their first serious rows, Shaun complained that she was prizing style over content. He accused her of preferring to have sex on a train to making love in his bed; to have done it, rather than to have felt it. He was right. He knew everything. She adored him.

And he was still pretty well the same guy. He was a lovely man. Gentle. Patient. *Quite* intelligent, though nowhere near as smart as she thought he was at first, when she idolised him. And he always was bloody petty. He asked her, after a while, to remove the nodding dog from the back window of her car. But she'd loved him for it, back then. She'd loved his irrational dislike for everyday things. These were the eccentricities that gave him his unique disposition, the human qualities that had made her want to be with him for ever.

She whittled down her list so that only two pertinent factors remained. One was that his accident had altered him – only subtly, but in a way that made him, to her, a different man to the one she'd loved so besottedly. She should have been more understanding about that, just as he had been with her, right from the start, but there was little she could do about it. And therein lay the second and biggest factor in all of this. Hilary. The great imponderable in this sad affair was Hilary herself. In five years she had almost totally reinvented herself. She'd gone from being a very immature twenty-year-old to a very accomplished – and impatient – twenty-five. She was different now. That was the top and bottom of it.

Lying on the beach, digging her toes down into the sand, this was what she now dwelt on. In the most basic terms she feared that she had simply grown apart from Shaun – or grown out of him. It was heart-wrenching, but she had to ask herself the question. Did she feel *anything* for her husband any more? That she could not give a definite answer spoke volumes, she thought.

Her mind was overheating in the deadly sun. She flicked at her book, but the white glare of the page blinded her. Bubbles of sweat formed rivulets in the tight furrow of her spine, trickling over her hip and down on to her towel. She hooked her bikini top back on and took herself down to the water's edge, conscious of the looks her small bottom was attracting from the older men. Perverts! She could have been fifteen, for all they knew!

She struck out into the sea, swimming after the silver trail of the sunlight. The shock of the cold water made her more abrasive, ducking hard into the waves and breathing deeply on the up until she acclimatised to the luxurious cool of the sea. She swam out further without looking back, enjoying a surge of excitement as she powered through the swell, getting out beyond the surf and into the inky cold slick of the deep. She thought of Madame Pontellier at the end of *The Awakening*, feeling a shudder of sisterhood. The aching purity of the pan pipes came back to her, soothing as she cut through the depthless ocean. She watched a gull let the wind toss it like a kite and thought again of Madame Pontellier and herself. She could only think that it was her lot to be so attuned to the melancholic.

She panicked momentarily when she eventually turned round. Her arms still felt strong, but she was miles out! The beach was just visible and the nearest soul was drifting along on a lilo way out of earshot. She let in the notion that she'd been swept out by an undercurrent and would now have to battle back feebly against the rip tide. Far away, one tiny white villa clung to the cliff. She kept it in sight as her marker as she commenced the long drag back.

She was slowing up, but making progress, too. The girl on the lilo was already coming into view. She could see now that she had red hair and a yellow bikini. Her back was going to be sore. A flaccid jellyfish flopped on the surface, ten or twelve feet away. Hilary tried to swim wide and past it but, her strokes weakening, she seemed only to invite the Hydrozoa closer. Her flailing breaststroke seemed to draw it inevitably in towards her until, just as she was bracing her flesh for the sharp sting of its trailing tendrils, she found herself staring into the mouth of a used and bloated condom. Someone was having fun at least.

Her mind settled to thoughts of Matt. Where did he

fit into all this? *Did* he fit in? She filtered out all but the core details. When she'd seen him on the plane, and particularly when they'd locked eyes for that second on the coach, she'd felt a jolt of something. She didn't think she was going to have an affair with him. She wasn't even certain of anything more than a rudimentary physical attraction for him. She'd agreed to go for a walk with him just because. She'd felt like it. She'd been in that sort of mood. Yet there was something powerful at work. From the start she'd felt the need in him. She didn't know if she wanted to find out what that need was.

She was getting back close to the breakers now. Other swimmers were further out than she was. She thought of Becky, studiously manipulating the atrophying backs and arms of her middle-aged clients. She felt lucky. She was lucky. She should just get on with it and see where the road took her. She swam into the shallows and stood up to wade the last few metres back to shore. The spuming suck of the surf knocked her off her tired legs and on to her backside. She lay back and let the gentle waves spill over her, enjoying the mesmeric regularity of their assault and retreat.

'Can you do me, Mikey, baby?'

Anke held out the buckled, near-spent tube of Bergasol. Mikey spoke to his newspaper.

'Can you get someone else to do it, hon? My hands are covered in sand.'

She watched him for a moment longer. She wasn't angry. She probably wouldn't have kept in touch with him anyway, once she got home. But, what had it been? Four days? Four days and he wouldn't get up from his fucking newspaper for her. He'd practically applied it with his mouth a day or two ago. Fuck him. No worries. She went over to ask Matt. She should have gone with her instincts and stuck around for old soulful eyes in the first place. Maybe she still would. Maybe not. None of it really mattered a great deal. It was all fine.

Hilary idled along through the shallows, scuffing her feet in the spray of the breakers. She found a quiet spot at the furthest end of the beach and spread out her towel. She sat down to watch the lissom Spanish girls playing ball games at the water's edge, next to a small precipice where their boyfriends cavorted and pushed each other into the clear green depths below. Only one or two of the girls were pretty, but all had lithe Kate Moss figures. Did the sunshine suppress their hunger, or did it merely melt away teenage puppy fat? She watched them leap and lunge and stretch for the ball, their supple spines rippling under taut skin. There was not a pick of spare flesh on any of them, yet a hundred paces away sat their heavy mothers and hirsute grandmas, indolent and resentful in their sinking deckchairs. If that was the transformation brought about by maternity then Hilary reckoned she'd rather stay celibate for ever.

And she had been celibate, really – for a long time. As she shook out her towel and made her way back along the waterline, she started to give birth to the idea that maybe she was no different to those girls, in a sense. She was, in some respects – certainly sexually – still quite artless. Perhaps a shrink would tell her she was nurturing a grudge against Shaun for stealing away her youth. Perhaps one wicked, crackling, completely thoughtless fling would get her over this gridlock in her mind. Perhaps it would actually help them. She found herself out with a smile – perhaps she was just looking for an excuse to shag young Matt.

So, having at last admitted to herself that she did, she *did* want to sleep with Matt, or somebody, somebody else, just once maybe, just to see, she was almost straight away chastened by the brevity of her new fantasy. As she picked her way up the beach, weaving around territorial baskets and towels, she almost tripped over Matt before realising it was him. He was with a crowd of other kids. There was a fat boy with bad sunburn who she presumed to be the philosopher, Pasternak. But she could only see Matt. Matt, who was rubbing sun cream into the tapering back of an elegant blonde. His look when he saw Hilary said it all. His mouth actually dropped open as he tried to stammer something or other, but she just walked on, trying to look blasé. That was that one then. She was, in a way, quite relieved to have had the decision taken away from her. Back from dreamland and, before long, back to work. Back to reality. She was starting to relish the prospect.

Shaun splashed his face and scalp with the mountain water and ducked his head to take a draught from the cool, iron-tinged stream. He was parched. He'd finished the last of the near-boiling water from his plastic bottle over by the ravine, figuring it would slake him until he got back. But the trail back through the foothills gave no cover from the high sun and he was gasping by the time he got down to the rivulet in the rocks. He caught his breath, swooped for more water, wiped his mouth and found a spot to sit by the riverbank.

To his side, lustrous big black ants scuttled around the oozing carcass of a crushed beetle. He was overcome with grief at the indignity, the squalor involved for both parties. He looked inside his sack for any broken bits of bread. His fingers found crisp crumbs of bread crust and a morsel of cheese. He scattered them around the beetle case and sat back to observe. The ants went into overdrive immediately, separating into breaking and carrying teams, chipping the crust down to a manageable size and dragging it away through a crack in the earth. The idea occurred to Shaun that he was sitting on a gigantic warren of ant tunnels and that underneath crawled teeming insect multitudes, colonies and colonies of industrious ants. He wondered how long it would take, if he had a solution that could gently strip away the soil, layer by layer, to get to the real substance of the ground. Ants. He took a final look at the last greying piece of cheese being borne to the underworld and got himself up again, ready for the hike across to Maro.

By the time he reached the viaduct he was thirsty again. It was after five, but the sun was still raging. From here back to the apartment would take another sluggish hour. He opted to continue downhill into the little village, have a beer at the bar and start the final leg once the worst of the heat had gone out of the day. His feet were sore. He smiled at the image of nuns kissing his livid soles as he tramped down the hill into Maro.

'Are you stalking me?'

He spotted her little jeep at the same time as he heard her voice. He looked up. Standing on the balcony of a pretty, whitewashed apartment was Maggie.

'What you doing there?'

'Erm, good question. What *am* I doing in the place where I live?'

'You live here?'

'I do.'

He felt foolish. He looked at his watch. 'What happened to Granada?'

'Couldn't fill the coach. Joined them up with another company.'

'Tremendous.'

He stood there, not knowing what to say.

'What makes you stray into Spain's most unfriendly village, anyway?'

'Really?'

'Oh yes! I keep asking my boss to include it in the Breakaway brochure. Come to Maro and be stared at by children, hissed at by hags and ignored by bar staff! Only 2,000 pesetas!'

He laughed and squinted up at her, smiling. 'I hadn't quite got that far, yet. I've been out walking in the hills. Just fancied a beer, really.'

She smiled back. 'Stay right where you are. You might stand a chance of getting served if I accompany you. Token incomer, I am. They no longer spit in my face. They merely stab me in the back now!'

'Wonderful!'

She was out there with him a minute later. To his surprise she took his hand as they walked. She clearly thought nothing of it, and he tried not to.

'How come you live down here?'

'Just happened, really. I've been here years.' She looked down past the convent and out to sea. 'I just decided to stay.'

They came to a tiny plaza, with benches looking out

over the olive groves that ran down to the cliff edge. She looked up at Shaun, as though snapping out of a dream.

'What about you, you weirdo? What sort of holiday are you having?'

'A weird one. But very nice, thank you.'

She raised her eyebrows. 'Fancy a drink, then?'

'Absolutely.'

They went into the little café opposite the church. Two old men played checkers at the table by the open door. At the bar, three younger men gossiped and guffawed loudly. Shaun expected them to stop talking when he came in, but they waved to Maggie as one continued with his anecdote and the others listened in disbelief.

Maggie chattered in Spanish with the bar owner, who kissed her hand and rubbed it where he'd just kissed her. He tried to give her back two 500-peseta coins for the 1,000 note she'd handed him. She wagged a finger at him, left one of the coins in the dish and led Shaun to a table at the far end of the bar.

'Cooler back here. And cheaper, did you know?'

'Wasn't sure, actually. I know they do it in France, but frankly – on holiday, you keep spending until it's gone, don't you? I mean, I'm not looking for a bargain, necessarily.'

'Ooh, well! I'll just shut up with my annoying tips, shall I?'

Shaun laughed and raised his glass. 'To useless information!'

She clinked and eyed him mischievously. 'So – how goes it with old jammy knickers?'

'She's fine.'

'Friends again?'

'Sure.'

'Which is why you're out yodelling and she's off trying to get rescued by the lifeguard.'

'She doesn't like mountains. I don't like lifeguards.'

'Made for each other, really, aren't you?'

He paused for thought before answering, drawing his breath as though he were about to speak, thinking better of it then, eventually, speaking very deliberately. 'Probably not. But then – I ask myself – who is?'

'Bloody good question,' she sighed.

He sat there with Maggie and told her a little bit about how he and Hilary had met. He spoke about the accident, about how he thought he was driving Hilary mad, but he didn't know what he could do about it. Whereas once all she had needed was his presence, now he felt it was best when he made himself scarce. Maggie kept quiet, listening, her turquoise eyes moist. When he stopped she hung her head for a while.

'I don't know what to say.'

'I don't suppose there's much *to* say. It's complicated. I'm on holiday with a woman who's thinking of leaving me.'

'How can you just sit there and say that?'

He was going to repeat it to see if it made her laugh, but he just shrugged instead.

'Because I sort of agree with her. It must be hard for her, hey?'

'Jeez! She could be a little more understanding, though!'

'No – it's gone beyond that, I think. I think she finds it distressing just to be with me.'

'What about her? Surely she has little things that drive you crazy?'

He stroked his chin and looked at the ceiling fan, half smiling.

'Hmm. Yes. She has this CD called *Feng Shui – Sacred Space*. I could cheerfully snap that in half.'

She smiled weakly. 'Be serious.'

'I am. I really despise that ethereal claptrap. I do.'

'But you don't despise *her* for it, do you? Maybe you think of it as being part of her? You think it's cute?'

'At best. Erm – what's it got to do with you, by the way? That's a serious enquiry. Why are you so interested?'

She gulped at her beer and looked directly into his Marty Feldman eyes. 'I don't know. I suppose I must like you, hey? Maybe I fancy you!'

He pulled a flabbergasted face. 'God! Don't go doing that!'

She cackled and clapped her hands. 'Don't worry yourself! You're safe! I made a vow a long time ago that I was not going to kill myself with men. But I still look out for the good ones. Maybe I'm just rooting for you, hey? I want you to be happy.'

'I am happy.'

'No. You're not.'

'Oh.'

He shrugged again, in a way that said 'Ah well. There we have it.' Maggie suddenly leaned forward, excited.

'Hey! You'll love this, though. This'll cheer you up! Tomorrow night, right, up at the caves . . .'

'The caves?'

'You must have seen signs? Las Cuevas de Nerja? Oh,

they're legendary – they're the most incredible forma-
tions – stalagmites and fossils and the other stalag things
that grow the other way up! Amazing! Totally stunning!
Anyone who can burst into tears at the sight of a
putrefying monastery will love it down there! Anyway,
even more so tomorrow. There's a classical guitar
recital, you know, candle-lit, dead atmospheric – it'll be
sumptuous, I promise you!'

He smiled and nodded. 'It does sound wonderful.
Can we get tickets?'

'We can. Will you be my date?'

'No hanky-panky?'

She offered her little finger to shake. 'Friends.'

'You're on.'

'Brilliant! There's a café above the caves. Nice patio
bar with a sun deck. Overlooks all this, actually. So – I'll
meet you out on the deck at seven. That OK?'

'More than. I honestly can't wait.'

He gave her a kiss on the cheek and, as he walked
back up the hill, wondered how long it would take for
her to hate him, or for him to hate her if they were to
start seeing each other.

Day Five

The metronomic thud of the headboard roused him first, then he became aware of the squalid heat before he fully realised where he was, what was happening. Shaun was dry-humping the mattress, fucking it remorselessly like he needed to squash a defiant frog with his pelvis. He'd been hammering the bed so hard that it had shifted right up against the wall so that the headboard was slapping out a relentless beat. Any passer-by would assume that violence, or violently energetic sex, was taking place. He rolled over, hair plastered all over his sticky, breathless face and tried to catch up with himself. He'd had such a powerful dream about himself and Maggie that to wake up now, without her, was crushing. Worse was his glad realisation that he was seeing her later and that he was in love with her. He had to talk this madness through with Hilary, but Hilary was gone again.

When he got back the night before Hilary had been fast asleep, naked on top of the bed except for a damp towel cooling her lovely back against the night air. He sat at the foot of the bed and watched her with joy. He started to stroke her spine and moved across so that he could kiss her fragile shoulders. No insect repellent to ward him off this time – just his own misgivings. If he were to pursue this lovemaking to conclusion, what would that make it? Was it in any sense at all a rape? He felt as though it was, and stopped. He looked up at the ceiling and lay and pondered without reaching any conclusion. He got up and wrapped some ice cubes in a face cloth, lying down on his back again and caressing his troubled brow with the cool bag. At some stage, his mind dull and aching, he passed over into a weak sleep. Lying there now the mattress was soaked through from the night's worries and the melted ice.

He showered and went out to find Hilary, imagining she'd be by the poolside. Only when he stepped outside the apartment into the shocking phosphorescent glare did he start to appreciate how long he had slept. It was the middle of the day. The towering white sun had already scalded the terracotta path red hot, so that he had to go back indoors for sandals just for the short walk to the pool.

In the midday mirage, the leaves of the lime trees looked like waving hands waiting to greet him as he passed. Ahead, a sprinkler doused the tumbling gardens. Shaun stepped back to let the roving spray gush past him. As he waited there he found himself wondering what difference it might have made if he had gone on and walked through the sprinkler's mist. He would already be up at the pool by now. Would he be leading a different life?

Hilary wasn't by the pool. He was curiously down-hearted by this, having no real plan of how he might spend the day. He missed her. He wanted to be with her or, at least, to be talking with her, getting somewhere, making some sort of headway with all of this.

He trudged back to the apartment. This was the hottest, clammiest day of the week so far. As slowly as

Shaun was walking, perspiration still ran freely down his forearms and shins. His polo shirt, possibly a size too brief in any case, stuck to his back and chest. This time he waited for the sprinkler to come around so that he could cool himself in its fresh spritzer. He thought about Maggie again and decided that perhaps he didn't love her so much as really, really like her. Whatever, he was looking forward to seeing her again.

Once again it was Pasternak's idea and again it seemed he was to be thwarted. The garage owner was having none of it.

'Too *grande*! Too *grande*!'

'Say what you mean, why don't you?' muttered Pasternak, dismounting from the creaking scooter.

The others were fine. Anke, Krista and Millie all rode scooters back in Nijmegen. They quickly convinced the proprietor they were no risk at all with a series of quick bursts and manoeuvres around the forecourt. Each of the three girls could carry a pillion passenger, which left only Pasternak, the fat bloke. At first he'd tried to blag the owner that he had his own scooter.

'Me Ace Face in Manchester, man. Me Stingo. Top Mod!'

'What sort scooter you got?'

He pulled an affectionate, dreamy face. 'Big gold scooter!'

The garage owner looked over Pasternak's profligate stomach, made up his own mind and flapped one dismissive hand at him. 'Save it for the chicks!'

'No, really! Ace Face! Top Mod!'

'What sort scooter?'

'Big gold Lamborghini.'

'Lambretta?'

'*Si*!'

He pointed to a nearby Li200. 'Show me. Ride.'

A minute later the front wheel of the scooter was wedged in the trough of a palm tree. The proprietor seemed to enjoy the fun as much as anyone. Putting his arm around the fretful Pasternak and escorting him back into his garage, he seated him on a simple but responsive Motoguzzi and gave him the three-step crash course. Within moments the Ace Face was leading his gang of four down the Autovieda de Atlantica to the water park at La Caleta.

Sipping at her piping-hot espresso on the little terrace high up in the village of Jatar, she couldn't help chuckling to herself. This was all Shaun had wanted. Always the simple things. If he'd been there with her, this would undoubtedly have been the highlight of his holiday. Poor Shaun. She thought about the note she was going to leave him, just to say that she was sorry she'd gone barmy and it wasn't his fault and she was working it out – but she'd screwed it up and burned it at the roadside when she got outside. It *was* his fault. She'd stood there at the bedroom door and watched him sleeping and felt nothing. *That* was his fault, and if it wasn't then it certainly wasn't hers. She did feel bad about treating him so wretchedly and she did want to sit down with him, soon, and talk it all out. But sorry as she was about the situation, she wasn't *sorry*. She didn't want a reconciliation. She didn't want to start walking backwards. To have left the letter would have implied grounds for reconciliation and there were none. She dabbed at her eyes with the napkin and left a 200 coin under the saucer.

She wandered around the silent streets, deserted at midday in the indolent heat of high summer. She seemed to gain the highest point of the village. There was a tiny graveyard on the mossy slopes directly above, accessible only by way of a crumbling goat track, but all the other streets and alleyways traipsed back downhill from where she stood. She found a shady balcony at the peak, trailing a haphazard path to a tiny white chapel below. Leaning over the balcony, she could now see the faraway haze of a shimmering, silent procession making sluggish progress up the winding track. Stooped old men in black jackets and black berets carried the coffin; shrouded women and children wearing black panta-loons and black ribbons trudged in their wake. Hilary felt compelled to watch, aware of her own voyeurism yet knowing they could not see her and would not for a long time. The tinkling bells of distant goats played out a soothing elegy on the drifting mountain zephyrs. She was about to turn and walk back to the car when the procession rounded the final bend and slowly, step by step, made its way up the steepest stretch.

Hilary stood, head bowed and eyes closed, feeling the indignant gaze of every one of them as she intruded upon the most basic intimacy of their private lives. She was a tourist, watching the villagers bury their dead. She could feel their muted rage, but kept her head hung low. She pressed her eyes tightly shut and when she opened them again, hoping the cortège would have passed her by, found herself looking into the coal-black eyes of a pretty little girl, five or six years old. The girl smiled at her and held out a flower, before her mother

yanked her wrist to keep her moving. The little girl
turned to look at Hilary again, eyes dancing. The coffin
drifted away, glinting in and out of focus in the gaseous
haze. She wiped her eyes and made her way to the car,
full of her own insignificance. Yet she felt lighter as well,
or at least less troubled than before. Again she could not
fathom it. She could only get inside the car and drive
towards the next bit. That was all she could do.

'FORE! LOOK OUT! FAT BLOKE COMING!'

Pasternak flew down the serpentine tube, his weight
giving him terrific momentum as he jackknifed against
the slick walls, boom-boom-boom-boom, unable to
scream as the skin of his back burned hard on the fast
abrasive chute, unable to catch his breath as it suddenly
threw him out and upwards, way above the towel-sized
bottle-green pool.

'Must-be-safe-must-be-safe-must-be-safe!' he chanted
inwardly, the giddy thrall in his guts making him scream
at the scintillating horror of the sheer drop down.
'AAAAAAGH! DEAD MAN . . .!'

The last words were lost as he plummeted into the
icy green depths of the salt-water induction pool. Down
and down and down he went, hearing the queer trill of
his own bubbles and soundwaves in his inner ear. He
was starting to dread that he would never bottom out
and start to rise again when suddenly the bursting blast
of cold fresh air knocked him breathless. He gulped it
down, shuddering and trying to breathe some more
when a flash of Anke's vermilion swimsuit shot into the
water next to him. Giggling, he waited for her to
surface and hugged her closely. Still, he put on a coarse

Northern accent. 'THAT WERE BLOODY BRILLIANT, WERE THAT!'

She laughed. 'Too scary for me. I'm gonna lie down on the decks and let men desire me.'

'Can I desire you?'

'Not as much as I desire you!'

'Oh, shucks! You're just saying that!' He feigned pushing her away and was surprised to feel her pinching his bum. 'Madam! Some decorum, I implore you!'

They swam to the side. Millie was already waiting on the sun terrace, looking pleased with herself. She hid something behind her back.

'Guess what I got for Pastikins?'

He looked eager. 'Chocolate?'

She wagged a finger at him, grinned and pulled the *Daily Mirror* from its hiding place. He was hugely pleased.

'Wow! Well done! Where'd you get that?'

'Some guy was gonna throw it in the bin. I just asked him if I could have it.'

'Cool!'

'He wanted a hundred pesetas.'

'No way!'

'No way. I'm pulling your cock.'

'I wish.'

She gave him a mournful look but didn't pursue it. The two of them settled down next to each other, Pasternak immediately delving into his tabloid.

'Look at your back! It's all scratched!'

'It's just a bit of abrasion from the water slides. You always get it.'

'No! It's too savage! You sure you didn't have some hot chick tearing you up, Pastie?'

He looked hurt at the suggestion. 'Certainly not! Look at Anke's back – she's got it, too!'

Millie chuckled at him and snuggled closer.

'You read up all the important events of the world, Patsy Kensit's boob job and so forth, and Auntie Millie will soothe away your *sex wounds* . . .' She prodded him affectionately and kissed his back. '. . . With some nice cocoa butter, yah?'

Pasternak nodded eagerly. 'Ooh yah, yah! Ooh very yah!'

She slapped him down and started working on him. He'd never had a girl lavish such close physical attention upon him. It felt marvellous. He had an immediate bonk-on and had to cast his eye over the Rugby League scores, in which he had zero interest, to prevent any seepage in the galleys. He pressed down as hard as he could to flatten his erection against the floor and flicked over the pages without taking in a word. He was going to come. He was going to bloody well come!

'Hey, stop! What was that?'

'What?' Instantly guilty, he took it that she'd spied his twitching end and was about to unmask him.

'Turn back a page . . .'

He flicked it back towards the sports.

'There!' It was the Encounters pages. 'Fantastic! Read them out, Pastie!'

Relieved and thankfully limp again, Pasternak was only too glad to oblige.

'Women Seeking Men or Men Seeking Women or what? Women Seeking Women? Men Seeking Goats?'

'You know I don't like that sort of talk, darling.' She slapped his back and leaned over his shoulder, pressing her breasts into him.

'Please, God, no, not again!' begged Pasternak.

'Go on! Anything!'

'OK. How about this? "*Cuddly blonde fortysomething, nice lingerie, OHAC, seeks NSTDS with GSOH, OINK for nights out/in, maybe more?*"'

Millie stared at the page. 'What the fuck does that mean?'

Pasternak laughed. 'The codes are all pretty standard. Everyone *always* asks for GSOH – Good Sense Of Humour. You'd have to, wouldn't you?'

'What about all the rest of it? Is this normal in England?'

'Perfectly.'

'It's madness! It's . . . unbelievable!'

'We're a pretty crazy bunch, you know . . .'

She shook her head and prodded him. 'Come on! Tell me – I'm kebobbed!'

'Save it for the chicks . . .'

She prodded him again, impatient.

'OK. Own House And Car, that's another pretty standard one. Er, what the fuck's this? NSTDS? TDS is usually Tall Dark Stranger. No Shortarse Tall Dark Stranger?' He slapped his forehead with his palm. 'Doh! Obviously – Non Smoker Tall Dark Stranger. And, er – Own Income No Kids, I think. Not asking for much, is she?'

'Cuddly? What is this?'

Pasternak cleared his throat and said in a barely audible voice, 'Big. You know. Fat. Loveable. Cuddly.'

Millie thought about it. 'So this is a fat, rich woman with dyed hair who wants a tall, good-looking stud with his own bread and no kids, yah?'

'Double yah.'

'What's in it for him?'

'Well, the Own Income bit is a sop. She's saying "I may be rich, but I'm nobody's fool. Pay your way, guys. Gold-diggers – forget it." But she doesn't mean it. She wants a young stud to come in and clean her out but her dignity won't let her say so. She's saying she's got a few bob, she's sexually voracious . . .'

'Where's it say that?'

'Nice lingerie. She's as good as hanging out the red light with that one.'

'Nice lingerie! My God! What an old slut!'

'I don't think so, you know. I can picture this girl all too well. Nearer fifty than forty. Desperately lonely. She'll take anything that's going. Don't you feel sorry for her?'

She didn't answer. When he cranked his head back over his shoulder, Pasternak found Millie looking at him strangely. There was serenity there and admiration, maybe. And there was love. She was looking at him with adoration.

'You really are a very special guy, huh? I don't know how a guy of twenty is this . . . *sensitive*!'

Jeepers! He sat up and turned himself around, ignoring the compliment. 'Hey! Let's do one ourselves! Let's write a Lonely Heart, a jarg one, right?'

'Jarg?'

'Fake. Bogus. We'll do a mad one, for a laugh!'

She shrugged, unsure. 'OK.'

'Come on, help me. Let's see. We want the opposite of what people usually say. Which is what they generally mean.'

'There you go again. Mr Philosopher Man.'

'Here we go – "*Fat Loser, 20, NSOH, NCHIOM, seeks absolutely anyone for sex. Anywhere.*"'

She laughed and clapped her hands. 'Translate, please!'

He did a Leo Getz voice. 'Okeh, okeh, okeh! Listen, will ya! Okeh – "Fat Loser, 20, No Sense Of Humour, No Car, House, Income or Mates seeks absolutely anyone for sex. Anywhere." It's bloody honest, isn't it?'

She gave him a little kiss. 'You crazy animal. If you weren't absolutely loaded I'd think you were describing yourself here! But you know you can have me anytime, huh? Anywhere.'

She tried to hold his gaze but his eyes flickered nervously and it was back to Leo Getz. 'Shtop teasing me, will ya!'

The breathless menagerie of Matt, Krista, Tom and Mikey came yelping over to them, full of the rampant mischief of the water slides. Tom's penis was sticking out from the gusset of his ridiculous poseur's thong, to the prolonged hilarity of Anke and Millie. Saved by the bell, thought Pasternak.

Hilary, back by the pool, was aware she was starting to burn but couldn't find the impetus to turn herself over. It felt nice just how she was. So what if she got a little bit burned? She'd be home again in a couple of days, back to life, back to reality – it would all just be another memory. But she was pleased when the too-blonde rep with the chunky calves came into her field of vision offering timeshare leaflets. It gave her a reason to sit up. She glanced over the picture-perfect fold-out brochure, which in itself was a novelty. Normally, the rep would have passed the leaflet to Shaun. Shaun would have binned it, unread, as soon as she disappeared from view. It didn't seem too bad an offer.

'*COLLECT YOUR FREE VOUCHER WORTH*
8,000 PESETAS'

'That's about thirty quid,' she thought. 'What do I have to do?'

'*MAKE YOUR WAY to Maribelle Beach Resort Sud where you will find the quality, luxury and elegance you have come to expect from Mirabelle resorts. Take a tour of our magnificent new resort and receive a voucher worth 8,000 Ptas. for use in one of our Mirabelle-recommended establishments. Restaurants, shops, beauty salons, golf courses — the choice is yours! Or if your time on the Costa is limited, why not join us for a cocktail on our breathtaking Balcón Mirabelle and view the show home nearby?*

[See back for full conditions of this offer]

She wasn't spectacularly interested in a meal for one at a showy Mediterranean timeshare, but she did find herself quite drawn to the idea of viewing the resort. She knew she wouldn't buy into the scheme. She didn't think she even liked the idea of timeshares. Time Share. Didn't sit well for Hilary at all. But there was no denying it – she was fascinated to know more about it. She wasn't exactly sifting through a clutch of alternative offers just now, either. Fuck it – she was going. She filled in her name and apartment number and went to hand it back to the surprised and delighted rep.

★

Shaun was happy enough out there on the terrace sipping beer with Maggie, watching the sun dissolve into the sea – but when they went down into the caves she was right. It was like nothing he'd ever seen before.

Heads ducked down in the low-roof passage, they made their way down damp steps, worn smooth and rounded at the edges. The smell, mingled with the rancid sweat of a thousand ogling tourists every hour, was mustier and more historic than in any old place he'd known. But nothing in the miasmic drag of the vapours and nothing Maggie had told him could have prepared Shaun for the toppling, other-worldly grotto which fell away beneath and around him. He stood still at the viewing point, knowing he was holding up the concert-goers behind, but unable to move on before he had tried to take in at least a sense of the cornucopia of crystals and pillars and stalactites – the sheer *age* before him. It was grotesquely beautiful, and made all the more stunningly supernatural by the licking silhouettes and shadow-play of the candles' flames, hundreds and hundreds of them, everywhere. Shaun's first thought was that the vast cavern resembled a scene from *Doctor Nemo* or even *Aliens*. If those great, sensual, religiose pillars of calcium had started to bleed right then, Shaun would not have blinked. He moved on down the steps, spotted the smiling eyes of a radiant Maggie and went to sit next to her.

She handed him a pamphlet explaining the ancient guitar music of the region, but when the short, pensive guitarist introduced his accompanying musicians and began to play Shaun recognised the style of the tune. It was 'Classical Gas' – or if not that, it was certainly the style of traditional scaling guitar upon which John Williams had based his more accessible version. Shaun looked it up in the programme: 'Asturias (1892)'.

That was all it said. It was magical. Shaun closed his eyes and let the lilting chords wash over him, seep through him and inside of him. He felt Maggie's thigh press up against his as a latecomer excused himself and squeezed past them. He kept his own thigh there, warm against hers, pushing gently against her as the guitars unpicked his cares. He cradled his neck on the shoulder rest and stared up at the mystical lights and shadows, blown this way and that by the quiet storm of the concert music. If a moment could be timeless or beyond time's grasp he felt this was it. He joined in the ripple of enthusiastic applause and closed his eyes again. A jaunty polka, it sounded like, followed by one or two more dissonant, experimental pieces. Then, from nowhere, he was taken aback by the craving, bittersweet introduction to the next track. It felt as familiar as a best-loved lullaby from childhood, reassuring yet sad, embalming him with the simple inevitability of its story. Yet he knew he had never heard this song before. Never. He snatched up the sheet again. 'Recuerdos de la Alhambra'.

Memories of the Alhambra. It was as unknown to Shaun as the wondrous palace of its title yet, as its haunting tremolo blew gently through his soul, he was able to shut his eyes tight and feel his way from chord to chord right through to its aching, romantic crescendo as though he had written the piece in his sleep last night. He gave way to it, breathed with the music and let the spirit of it drain deep down inside him, then he pressed his leg tightly against Maggie's warmth.

★

'YES! YES! YES! OH YAH! OH, MOST DECID-
EDLY OUI, OUI, OUI!'

The others ignored him and kept on walking through
the shade of the narrow streets.

'Soo-perb! JUST buh-brilliant!'

Mikey wandered back and brush-clipped the top of
his head with his flat hand. 'What the FUCK are you
rattling on about?'

Pasternak, eyes gleaming, pointed at the poster. 'We
have to go! We HAVE to attend!'

The others ambled back and took turns looking at the
badly photocopied fly-poster in the big bar window.
Matt read it out. '"Bar Narranja is pleased to aknown
the retorn of Eve Y Christophe and they award-
winning *ABBAESQUE* cabaret chow. Fituring all your
favorite hits!"'

Pasternak turned to them, arms out wide in a what-
did-I-tell-you mode. 'We HAVE to be there.'

The girls took no persuading.

'I'm there!'

'Me also.'

Tom, more modest now in khaki shorts, showed his
big, flat, disdainful front teeth. Just once or twice Matt
had really wanted to sock him one because of those
teeth. Not that he had anything much against Tom –
just his teeth did his head in when he was acting spoilt.
He was doing it now and Matt felt like cracking him.
The surly teeth came out at the same time as the
complaining, soft, only-child whine.

'*Ab*-bah! Who's interested in bloody Abba?'

Pasternak looked at him in amazement. 'I'm not even
going to dignify that with a response. If you don't get it,
you don't get it. But this, mark my words, is going to be

one of the highlights of your holiday. This has just dropped right out of the skies into your very lap. It's from heaven, man! This is from heaven! It's going to be amazing!'

Krista limbered over and took Tom's hand. 'Hey, he's right. It's going to be great fun.'

Tom took out his anger on his beautiful, peaceful, much taller girlfriend. 'Abba!' He wrenched his hand free. 'Suit yourselves!' He stormed off up the street, stopping to shout, 'If I'd known we were coming on a disco-kitsch holiday I'd have saved my money and gone to Flares instead!'

The worst thing they could have done was laugh, but the sight of his angry red face hollering those words creased them up. Tom stood there, not a violent boy but overheating now and on the verge of a tantrum. He threw his head back dramatically, making himself more ridiculous as he took deep breaths to control himself. He glowered at them, eyes blazing. 'KIDS!'

He strode off. Krista went to go after him, but Mikey stopped her.

'Leave him for a few minutes. He'll be fine.'

She looked shocked. 'Where did that come from?'

Pasternak stepped forward, pinching his nose to give his voice a reedy, intellectual timbre as he began a rapid-fire commentary. 'He feels betrayed by you. He's never loved anyone like this in his life, never felt this way at all. He's found himself slipping out of control, power-less, obsessed. He just wants it to be him and you, him and you all the time. He feels compromised every time you share yourself with us. Every beach picnic, every boat trip, every disco night is just more time lost to poor Tom – time he could have you to himself, dear Krista.

We only have a few days left. He can't believe he's with someone as fantastic as you and deep down he doesn't feel worthy of you. He certainly doesn't believe for a minute that you'll remember him when you get back home to Holland. He's a hopeless, but not unusual case, I'm afraid. You'll have to go easy on him. Thank you.'

He gave a little bow and stepped back. Everyone just looked at the funny fat boy for a moment. Millie shook her head in astonished admiration. 'He's right, of course.'

Krista nodded. 'I should have seen this. Oh dear, oh dear!'

Mikey, laughing, started to clap. 'Congratulations, Doctor Freud!' Malevolently, he turned to the others. 'If you could now just apply similar intuition to your own strange case perhaps we'd all be getting somewhere.'

Pasternak, knowing Millie's eyes were upon him, tried to fight down the flush of inadequacy he could feel rising up. For a second he was exposed – but only for a second.

'All you need to know about me, Mikey Boy, is that I'm going to be here, tonight, waving my hands in the air like I just don't care! That's me, Mikey. The good Doctor Fun.'

Matt smiled and winked at him. Mikey made a sly face to himself, indicating that he and Pasternak knew better. They went to find Tom.

Maggie snuggled her back against the wooden fence of the viewing deck and watched him, so wild, so lost. He shuddered once more.

'Feeling better now?'

He turned his gaze away from the sparkling ocean. 'Much. It was just . . . beautiful. Like you said – sumptuous.'

'I've never seen a man cry like that before.'

He looked at her full on. 'I do it often. It seems to do the trick for me, letting things out, things that are trapped inside. But that wasn't sad crying, just then. That was just . . . wonderful. All of it.'

He drifted off over the sea again. She followed his eyeline out to the crumbling old watchtower on the headland overlooking Maro. She turned to face him, stood up on her toes to wipe away a tear. She looked into his eyes and seemed to come to a decision.

'I want to show you something,' she said. 'Come on.'

Even in the little jeep with its four-wheel traction, they were driving down the dirt track almost at right angles. Shaun had to tuck his head right over to the driver's side as the Vitara scraped past bushes and brambles and dry, crackling leaves. Shaun's side of the vehicle seemed two feet lower down than Maggie's. The steep track was heavily rutted down the middle, causing the imbalance. On Maggie's side was a sheer drop of three or four hundred feet down to the olive groves and hothouses full of tomatoes and grapes below. On Shaun's side it was a steep, bush-clad embankment leading to the pine-strewn headland and the squat, sedentary watchtower. They scrambled round another scree bend and the dirt track shallowed out into a small plateau enclosed by trees. That was the end of the road. Beyond was a drop down to the sea.

They sat still in the Vitara, engine running. Maggie gulped hard and rocked forward slightly. She seemed to be steeling herself, or trying to find the courage to make the next move. Shaun decided to say nothing. Even in the muggy calm of the hilltop evening, the shrill crack and spit of the cicadas tore the greasy air. It felt like rain was coming.

Directly ahead were two twisted yew trees whose branches had knotted together over the years. Beyond them was a slight drop to a clearing and a smaller yew and, under its boughs, a small marble bench seat. Shaun got out of the car and paced very slowly over to the marble bench, resting a foot upon it and cupping his chin in his hand, elbow propped up on his raised thigh as he surveyed all around. A metre from the bench was the drop down to the sea. Directly up above them was the watchtower, built centuries ago to warn of invading hordes of Moors, Phoenicians, Genovese. Shaun smiled. It was the Brits, the Germans, the Scandinavians now.

As he stepped back from the bench, a glint of something caught his eye. Just in front of the bench was a plinth, a memorial stone. *En memoria de Denis Thompson. 6.5.1919–19.9.92.*

He bowed his head.

'That's what gave me the idea.' He hadn't heard her approaching. 'I used to come up here all the time. Ages ago.'

She took him by the hand and led him along a trail, barely passable, dropping steeply and dramatically this way and that until they came upon a small plateau. Squinting against the ghostly twilight, he could just about make out a narrow track weaving all the way down to the small beach, but this really was as far as anyone could safely go.

★

'MONEY-MONEY-MONEY, AH! AIN'T IT FUNNY, AH! IN A RICH MAN'S WORLD!'

They surrounded Pasternak on the dance floor, waving peseta notes at him, ruffling his hair and jostling the dancing fool. Pasternak was really going for it, arms rotating backwards as though he were swatting imaginary flies off the tips of his ears as he let rip to the Abba classic. He'd been singing along as lustily as anyone until a couple of songs ago, but the tempo of 'Waterloo' followed by the equally bouncy 'Gimme Gimme Gimme' had put paid to the last of his stamina. He was getting by on carefully regulated good old-fashioned oxygen now. He needed to save some energy for later.

He looked around with satisfaction. Everyone was dancing, smiling, laughing, sweating and singing along to the undisputed champions of Eurocheese. Tom and Krista, when they weren't kissing hungrily in the centre of the crowded dancing area, were perfecting the one dance that seemed to suit their mood – Tom standing behind her, hands on her hips, humping her backside as she bumped and ground it back into his groin. Pasternak thumbs-upped him. Tom made a fingers-down-throat gesture but grinned back wildly, having the time of his life. Millie stood to the side taking snaps of her dishevelled pals, all going for it madly, whistling and cheering. Eve y Christophe had rarely known such an over-appreciative audience, but they were loving it. The enthusiasm of Pasternak and Co. infected everyone else, a mainly older crowd attracted by the two for one Sol offer and the six until midnight happy hour. Within three songs Pasternak had got all the women up, clapping along and giggling self-consciously until they realised how easy it all was. Pasternak jumped up and down in the midst of them, fist punching the air triumphantly. He'd done it again. He'd got them all going. He was indeed Doctor Fun.

His crowning glory was to follow soon after a tearful Eve y Christophe took their third bow, reluctant to have to leave this adoring throng and take up their final residence of the night at a club up the road. As Christophe broke down his drum machine and keyboard, Pasternak sidled over to him and whispered something. Christophe seemed only too delighted to be approached by the big fan and pointed over to the microphone. He put his keyboard back on its stand to the side of the dance floor. Seconds later, Pasternak had mounted the small stage. Those who were already crowding the bar to get their orders in before midnight started to turn back, already laughing at the sight of the big lad up onstage.

'Lay-deez and ah-gennel men! The lovely Eve and the fantastic Christophe . . .' He broke off until the spontaneous applause and whistling died down. 'Eve and Chris have entertained us magnificently tonight, I think you'll agree . . .'

More cheering and stamping of feet. Shouts of 'Get off, fatso!'

'I will, I will – I promise. But first let me try to put right the one oversight of an otherwise perfect Abba-esque set. Please join me in, er, enjoyment of this last Abba masterpiece. Thank you.'

Christophe started up a mewling approximation of the intro music. Pasternak gulped and gripped the microphone hard as he fell into his comfortable Barry White sway. He could see the girls holding their arms aloft, beaming proudly at him from the front row. He could hear the whistles and catcalls.

'Go on, Pastie! Go on my son!'

His friends looked thrilled. Their faces showed disbelief that anyone they knew could be this daring. He smiled to Eve, shimmying next to him, ready to come in with the backing vocals. Christophe, a tear in his eye, nodded to the fat boy. This was it.

'*I don't wanna talk/About the things we've been through . . .*'

A cyclone of appreciation nearly knocked him backwards as his friends and fans rushed the stage, arms and legs everywhere, fluorescent teeth, hair in the air, everyone dancing, flailing, throwing themselves into the song. It was like a punk rock concert. Pot-bellied men in their forties left their bottles of Sol on the table and ran to join in. Pasternak sang on passionately, unable to hear himself but knowing instinctively that he was hitting his notes. By the time he got to the chorus the tiny stage was overrun with joyous revellers, all trying to hold on for the big chorus. When it came Pasternak – ecstatic, tearful – threw his head back and bellowed out the words with an edge and a fury that took him by surprise:

'*THE WINNER TAKES IT ALL . . .*'

'Nah-nah-nah,' sang the happy crowd, filling in with Eve.

'*NOW IT'S HISTORY!*'

He saw Millie's small hand reaching for him. He could feel his voice starting to fail. He handed the microphone to the nearest willing chorister and jumped the short drop down to the floor. He pulled Millie back from the crowd, pulled her close to him and kissed her with all the force he could muster.

'Goodness me,' she said, licking her lips. 'That was nice. Do it again!'

And he did. He could do no wrong.

She sat down. He joined her. She looked straight ahead and, in a trance, indicated a cluster of small, perfectly round stones to her right. A tiny cross was embedded at the peak.

'That one's mine.'

He went to get up, but she held him firm.

'Let me tell you. I want to tell you.'

'Yes. Please.'

He heard clearly each and every shift of mood as she told it to him.

'Can you imagine it? When I first came here I'd spent almost the entire winter on a sunbed!' She laughed bitterly. '1986. Me and my ma bought it together out of the catalogue. Four-tube, swivel-hood Philips job — we thought we were it! Used to charge the neighbours to use it. When I finished my O levels and came out here with the girls I was just this orange thing. I *was* orange. It was the only suntan I'd ever had. I thought I was gorgeous.'

The way her voice cracked on *gorgeous* made him want to hold her close. But he sat still and listened.

'It was much more of an 18–30 type resort back then. Bananarama skirts, slim wee thighs, Mel and Kim — I can sing every fucking word of every song to you.'

'What happened?'

'My own fault. I was desperate to be the first to bag off with a waiter. We all were. That was the be-all and end-all. Can you imagine? A fucking Spanish waiter? I don't blame them for the way they were. We were all over the poor bastards. We made it easy for them.'

Shaun nodded.

'I got off with this guy. He was actually called Manuel. We were laughing all week about it. I never thought I could love anyone as much as I loved Manuel, with his little wispy moustache and his bad teeth. When I came back to tell him I was pregnant they all closed ranks. Manuel? We don't know no Manuel!' She laughed bitterly. 'Who's the joke on now, hey?'

He shook his head. 'Yet you stayed?'

'I just decided to, just like that. I don't know what happened, whether it was, like, a sudden wee case of the *dolores* but before I knew it I was pouring blood, I was in hospital, I'd lost the baby.'

Shaun looked across at the pile again. A grave, then. Maggie, seemingly over the hardest part, was in control again.

'I had no insurance to pay the medical bills. I was a disgrace to my family – to *myself* – and I just decided I'd stay here. Me and the baby. Don't worry, she's not there. The hospital wouldn't let me have her. I had to pay to find out whether she was a boy or a girl. It was fucking horrible . . .'

Shaun leaned across and pulled her to him, holding her in his powerful arms. 'Come on.'

She gave a little laugh. 'I'm fine. I wanted you to know all this. I wanted somebody . . .' She broke off and looked out to sea and this time she *was* in tears, though still laughing. '. . . to know about me.'

'Jesus Christ.'

She laughed. 'Exactly. And then I stumbled across

this place. It's just . . . *alive* with ghosts, don't you think?'

Shaun nodded.

'So I made my peace, made my little memorial and just . . .' She took a deep breath. 'You know. Here we are. I got my place down the hill, right where I could be with my baby. And I just settled into it. At first I thought I was Joan of Arc, snooping round after young girls on holiday, trying to stop them from shagging the local harpoons. That's what you reminded me of that first time I saw you. You were on a mission. There was no way, in your mind, that you were doing *anything* out of the ordinary. I saw that straight away. That was me. I used to let myself into the girls' apartments and place condoms by the bedside. I nearly got the sack.'

She took a deep breath and shook her head. 'After a while, though, all that left me, you know?'

She looked at Shaun. He nodded. The freckles on her nose stretched and moved as she spoke. He really wanted to kiss her.

'I didn't feel so . . . *robbed*. I was still only eighteen. I could speak near-perfect Spanish. So I really went for it. I push punters into certain bars that give me a kickback. Same with car hire companies and coach excursions. There's a little bit in it for me from every sale, you know? And I started getting in on the property boom, second homes and all that. I was even dealing a few tablets up until a few years ago – just to make sure the kids got the good ones.' She nuzzled into Shaun. 'And that's it. That's me. I'm a red-heid from Dunbar who lives out here now.'

She shrugged. He squeezed her tightly to him. She felt it was supportive, more than passionate, so she didn't fish for a kiss. She hugged him back. He got up and walked to the very edge of the precipice. She came to join him, looping her fingers through his belt fobs. Shaun leaned back into her.

'Can I ask you something?'

'Sure.'

'What did you call her?'

She was silent for a moment.

'Bonita.'

'That's lovely.'

'That was the song, you know? When we girlies were out here on holiday, all so young and gorgeous and . . . *free*. We were free. And that's what we were dancing to, us beautiful young creatures. "La Isla Bonita". Freedom.'

She pushed off from him and took up her own spot on the edge of the cliff.

'But you're free now, hey? You're an outlaw. If you're not free then nobody is.'

She thought about it. 'I need a man, though. So I'm not free, am I? I need a man.'

He couldn't look at her. Like a gauche adolescent, he didn't know what to do. He could feel her looking at him, willing him to come over. When she spoke again there was a certain sting in her voice.

'There's another reason why I stay out here, too.'

'What's that?'

'I really couldn't tell you.'

'Try.'

'It would be so much better if you'd let me show you instead.'

'When?'

'It's my day off tomorrow.' She'd been talking to the

encroaching dark, but now she turned to face him, brighter. 'I'm sorry for prattling on. I know what you're going through. Just know that I'm here for you, right?'

He smiled.

'As much or as little as you need.'

'Thanks.'

She shot him a cute look. 'I was only trying to nab you while you were still vulnerable. Can't blame me for that, hey?'

He laughed out loud, making her laugh, too. She came over and took his hand and walked him back to the jeep.

'Set your alarm, yeah? You won't regret it. I'll meet you up by the telephone boxes at eight, right?'

'Right.'

As he slammed his passenger door shut he felt a sensation he hadn't had for weeks. It was the convulsive shudder of his spine against the cold. Or perhaps it was fear.

He could feel her woozy affection, feel her eyes on him from the other side of the room. He stayed where he was, pottering around in the kitchenette, pretending to fix snacks and drinks for everyone. She was trying to look sultry. Pasternak didn't think it suited her – she looked like a well-made Brooke Shields in *Pretty Baby* when she tried to look sultry. He sneaked a quick glimpse over at her. Shit! Looked her straight in the eye! What he saw in her eyes was love. Big love. Fuck! He was going to have to deal with this. Sooner or later, it was going to come to the crunch. The others would pair off, go back to the Nijmegen apartment as usual. Matt would go to bed. And that would leave him and

Millie, all alone. Randy, rampant Millie, on fire now that Pasternak had declared his feelings in Bar Narranja – she'd wanted his body from the start and now she thought tonight was the night. The Big Night.

'Yo! Pastie! What's happening with the drinks, man?'

He found himself rooted to the spot, frozen by the fridge door. This was his last chance. If he set foot out there, if he left the succour of the little kitchen, he was dead. There would be no turning back. He was going to have to sleep with Millie. Shit, shit, shit, shit, shit! How he wanted to! How he couldn't!

He lurched out with a big, daft grin on his face. 'Ooh ah wah-wah, bag bah-wah-wah!'

They started laughing, unsure. 'What? What's he saying?'

Pasternak began laughing dementedly, laughing and pointing at Matt. 'Ooh bah-wah-wah!'

'What?'

'He's pissed,' said Matt.

Millie's face dropped. 'He wasn't so bad just now. When we all walked back.'

Pasternak rolled his eyes and managed to make himself foam at the mouth. Matt jumped to his feet. 'Shit! I've seen him like this before. He just goes!'

He snapped his fingers to illustrate. Pasternak could have hugged him.

'Nice work, mate,' he thought. 'I owe you one.'

Matt marched him through to the bathroom and pushed his head over the basin.

'Not so rough,' thought the fat lad. Miraculously, Pasternak found himself able to produce copious amounts of sick. He was puking to order. Matt, dear Matt, wiped him down with a cold towel and escorted him to the bedroom. Moments later he was back with a dry towel and a bowl.

'There you go, matey. You sleep it off. I don't know if you can hear me, but there's a bowl by your side if you need to throw up in the night. And there's a glass of water by the bedside lamp. Have a good one.'

He closed the door. Pasternak smiled to himself. Result! He turned over, actually quite tired now, and listened to the conferring hum of their voices out there, all talking about him. He wasn't there and he was still the centre of attention.

He slept like a baby walrus, so he didn't stir one wink when she slipped into bed beside him. He didn't feel her naked breasts against his back as she reached around his waist to find his cock and he didn't feel her stroke it patiently, stroke it and pull it with all the love in the world. He didn't feel her warm lips and the gulp of her throat as she took him inside and he didn't hear her sigh of defeat as she gave up on the inert drunkard. Or he pretended not to, at least. As she kissed him so gently on the back of his shoulder and said, 'Sleep good, Pastie baby,' she couldn't have known that his eyes were wide open, staring blankly at the verandah door.

Day Six

She'd showered and dressed an hour ago and still they hadn't spoken a word. He was still sitting out on the balcony, feet up on the wall, looking out to sea. They'd made eye contact once, when she came out to get a towel. Shaun just looked resigned, regretful – sad, really. She hadn't expected it of him. She hadn't thought that hard about Shaun's side of it, but her instinct was that he'd go into denial, shrug it off like the child singing loudly to drown out the sound of his parents' fighting. Last night, anticipating this moment, she'd had a series of complicated arguments in her head with Shaun, all of which she won. At the outset of all these imagined arguments, though, he contributed to his demise by bouncing into the bedroom with a breakfast tray and waking her up with a jaunty 'Hello, stranger!'

That was really what she thought he'd do – or perhaps it was merely what her subconscious hoped he'd do. If his first words to her in three days of silent misery and consternation were 'Hello, stranger', then he'd deserve the mauling she was ready to give him.

But he didn't. He said nothing. He was neither hostile nor welcoming – he just went out on to the verandah and sat there. Now Hilary wanted to sit and talk with him – at least get started on the business of breaking down this boulder between them and getting a look at what lay ahead – but the longer the silence went on, the harder it was for her to do something about it. She lingered by the patio doors, watching him. His long hair rested on his shoulders, the same length it had always been. Shaun only rarely had the very ends snipped but his hair never seemed to get any further down his back. She'd always loved his golden hair. And his back.

Overcome with sympathy for him and chastened by a parallel self-disdain, she went to the fridge and poured two glasses of orange juice and pulled up a chair next to Shaun.

'Hi.'

She almost said 'Hi there, stranger', but pulled herself up short. His reply rocked her back.

'It looks bad, doesn't it? Looks like we're over.'

She couldn't take it in. This was what she had been telling herself all week; this was the future she was steeling herself for. Yet when he said it, it was nothing. It was shocking, but it was like he was talking about someone else, two people not themselves. When she thought about it again later, she could only liken it to the day her uncle had come to pick her up from school and, in the back of his car, told her her father had died. Like Shaun, he broke it into two parts. 'Daddy's had a heart attack. He's gone, darling.'

That, she could only hazard, was what gave these moments their air of unreality. Although the message imparted was final, some oblique signal contained in the first part gave her subconscious something to cling to. When Uncle Alan told her about Daddy, she didn't come to understand for hours that there was no reprieve. She still saw herself rushing to his hospital bed and finding a flicker, a sign that everyone else had missed. But it was useless, of course. She felt like that now. She'd spent days on her own, fantasising about a life away from Shaun, planning for it. Yet when he said it to her she was stunned.

'Is that what you want?'

He hardly paused. 'I think it is, yes.' Only now did he turn to look at her, softening a little. 'Don't you think it's best?'

She dropped her head. 'I don't know.' She felt cheated. After all that, it was. *him* dumping her!

The bizarre thought came to her that, if she was sitting on the other side of him, his earpiece side, this would be easier. Ridiculous!

He stood up and drained his drink. 'I do. I think it's all too obvious. It's very, very sad, but –' He ran his fingers through her still-wet, spiky hair. '– it's reality.'

She took his hand and kissed it. Tears wet her eyes. To her surprise and considerable hurt, Shaun took his hand away.

'I think it's dishonest of you to do that, now.'

She blinked back the tears. 'What?'

He looked stern. 'Think how you were in Ante-quera.'

She glared at him. 'You really hate me, don't you?'

'If only it were that easy. For you.'

'Bastard!'

He shrugged and walked back into the apartment.

'Where the fuck are you scuttling off to now?'

The front door opened and closed. Hilary sat there, feet against the wall, pushing the front legs of her chair back and forward, angry tears stinging her eyelids.

Upstairs, Darren, who had not long been asleep, turned

his head away from the balcony and buried himself under his pillow. His mouth was putrid. His head was rocking with each murderous pulse to his brain.

'Bastards! Noisy fucking bastards! Wish those fucking yuppies'd argue somewhere else! It's eight o'clock in the morning! Selfish cunts!'

As he reached the last flight of steps a cloudburst of emotion took him over. Had that been him, back there? How could he have done it to her? Little Hilary. Had he really said those things?

He shook his head. Yes – he'd said them and meant them. He'd just cut through it all and said it and got out. She'd be fine. He was giving her what she wanted. He was giving her back her youth.

He dragged the back of his wrist across his face to mop up the perspiration and take care of any solo tears. He took a deep breath and started up the steps. He didn't have any strict notions about this friendship with Maggie. He was drawn to her and she seemed to want to understand him and he needed that. There was no harm in it. Hilary could not, with any good conscience, complain about the way things were turning out. This was what she wanted – and she was right to want it.

Maggie was already waiting in the little Vitara, looking at a map. When Shaun caught her eye she gave him an extraordinary, huge smile and stood up to wave to him. He felt good, too. He found energy in his feet and bounded over to the car, vaulting in with one impressive hop. She clapped and pecked him on the cheek and started up the engine.

'Where we going? Come on, come on – tell me!'

'Steady!' she laughed.

He started poking her in the ribs and tummy. 'Tell me!'

'I'll tell you when we get there. Be good, now. Sit back and enjoy the ride.'

He leaned over and kissed her gently on the neck. 'Thanks,' he said.

She seemed pleased, but tried not to show it. 'What for?'

'For coming to my rescue. Thanks!'

She flapped a hand at him. 'Behave!'

He sat back and enjoyed the wind in his hair. They turned off at Almuñécar and started the climb up to the mountains.

Pasternak felt wretched. He was doomed. He was just – a *failure*. The girl he fancied, the girl who, let's face it, he was in love with, had got into bed with him to seduce him. All he had to do was . . . *do*. But he hadn't. He'd lain there like a big, scared jellyfish, pretending to be comatose until this morning when she had to get dressed and leave. What a loser! What a *failure*. He hated himself and he wanted to die.

Matt came to check up on him. 'I told the others we'd meet them down the beach.'

'Uugggghh!'

'You up to it?'

Pasternak used his most feeble voice, the one he used to call upon to convince his mother he couldn't go to school when it was football. 'Think I'll sleep it off,' he croaked.

'Sure. Well. You know where we'll be, yeah?'

Matt closed the door. Pasternak looked at the wall. He knew this for certain – he would never get a better chance again. She was sexy, lively, clever, funny, patient and she *adored* him! There *was* no problem!

He groaned and rolled over. He had two nights left. Two nights to think of something.

Hilary didn't like the guy at all. What was it with these Spanish businessmen? Was there a conspiracy that they all had to look like David Suchet? The bloke from the car hire firm, the little man in charge of the complex, the cashier at the bank yesterday and now this creepy timeshare guru with his dark, staring eyes and his neat moustache – each of them had been bald, lecherous and beautifully dressed. None had been much taller than five foot. Twice, now, Hilary had been sure the guy had tried to touch her breasts with his pate.

'No pressure, madam, is big decision and is necessary think hard about such big commitment. But remember, too – only thirty-three beautiful luxurious duplex apartments remaining and more people arriving to view every day. I don't have to sell. These place – they sell themselves.'

Hilary nodded as she had done throughout. At first she'd tried to seem perky and interested, asking questions and looking inside cupboards. But the pervading gloom of the morning took hold of her properly and by the time he showed her the gymnasium and swimming pool complex, she was in the throes of depression. This was not for her. This was a ritual for couples, for families, for lovers. A second home under the Mediterranean sun – not a likely prospect for a forlorn divorcee. She trudged along in his wake, nodding when he addressed her, but really thinking: 'Who buys these places? How much thought goes into it? What *is* a timeshare? What happens when you sign up on the spur of the moment and you move out here and you wake up one morning and suddenly you live in Torrox or Rincón? Do you just go down to the shops for some milk and a newspaper, same as you would do if you still lived in Ashton-under-Lyme? How much real thought and choice and planning goes into acquiring such a timeshare, before you actually go for it and take the plunge and change your life and come and live in another place?'

She found herself laughing. As much choice and planning as goes into the other big timeshare we enter into, she mused. The dapper little manager was pleased he'd made her smile.

'You like? You think you might like, perhaps?'

She smiled at him. 'I think I might like. Perhaps.'

She declined his invitation for a cocktail on the balcony and went back to the hire car. She was going to have to drop it off today. So soon. So soon. Edging her way out of the Mirabelle complex and into the main flow of traffic, Hilary noticed the resort's parade of specialist shops. Among the beauticians and pet-grooming parlours and tarot readers was a German psychiatrist. The services available were all notated in German, but she could make out that Dr Schoen was a very well-qualified analyst. If there was demand for a German shrink, why not a natural treatments and remedies spa? Why not?

In between the villages of Venta de Rica and Venta del Fraile, Maggie took a sharp turn to the right and skidded up a scree-bound track, juddering and jerking up an impossible gradient, so steep that, when Shaun looked back, it seemed certain that the jeep's grip would fail and they'd go careening back down to their deaths. The track cut abruptly to the right and from there took a more gentle route up through the forest. Goats watched in silence as they passed, then carried on tearing at the grass. As the forest began to thin out, a wolf came scrambling from the trees and boulders and chased the Vitara, chased them for half a mile growling at Shaun through slavering teeth. He laughed, but he was worried for a while.

Strobe beams of sun slatted through the flitting trees, throwing jagged light patterns in their path. Maggie winked at Shaun. 'This is it.'

He was about to ask more when the track funnelled out into a perfectly flat, loose scree cul-de-sac, shelving gently down to the mountain slopes. Shaun laughed. It was freezing up here. He thought it was just the wind gushing through the open-topped car, but now they were stationary it was colder still.

'Where are we?'

'Where are we, he asks! On top of the fucking world!'

She jumped out of her side, ran around to the back of the jeep and opened up the panel behind the spare wheel. Shaun got out to help. Maggie dragged out a large purple rucksack, almost half as tall as she was.

'What the ruddy heck?'

She laughed and shushed him. 'All will become apparent.' She looked all around her, laughing excitedly. 'This is perfect. These conditions are just so perfect. We'll have to hurry, though. We want to get the most out of these thermals while they're in our favour.'

'Shall I just nod?'

'Please.'

She struggled with the rucksack and started to empty out a huge yellow counterpane and spread it out flat on the hillside. Shaun wandered off to peer down the slope. She shouted after him. 'I wouldn't, if I were you.'

'Why not?'

'I'll tell you in a mo. Just get back here and give us a hand.'

She went back to the Vitara and threw him a padded, one-piece windsuit, like a protective ski outfit, but much thicker. He started to undress but she signalled no, it goes on over your clothes. It was surprisingly easy to slip on. One zip divided it like a sleeping bag, with two more zips on the insides of the salopettes sealing in all his body warmth. She thumbs-upped him and returned to the giant parachute, where she was fixing two little strap seats, like baby slings, to the main frame.

'Gets pretty cold up there,' she said as she worked, pulling on various wires and snap clips to test their tension. It took Shaun a while to digest.

'Er, up there?'

'Up there.'

'I mean – what you on about? I thought maybe you were into flying big kites, or something. I was all set to humour you for an hour then meet you back down in the village for lunch.'

Maggie, still fiddling with a thick nylon cord, looked up at him over her shoulder. 'If I'd have told you yesterday that we'd be flying six thousand feet over the earth's surface with nothing but God's wind to power us, you wouldn't have come, would you?'

She actually saw him gulp as he took in the information.

'Would I fuck!'

She laughed. 'Well, buddy. This is the other reason I live out here. Paragliding. Not commonly available in the Greater Lothian area.'

His mouth was wide open. 'Paragliding.'

It was as much as he could do to repeat the word, parrot-fashion. Maggie was radiant, like a missionary spreading the good word.

'Nature's own orgasm, I promise you. I got into it just after the baby died. These hippies took pity on me and brought me up here, let me in on their secret. You know people sometimes talk about the day that changed their lives? That was mine. You can't begin to appreciate it until you've been up there – but it does change your perception of things. You can reach out and touch heaven.'

Shaun must have looked like a ghost, grinning stiffly and nodding, wanting to go along with it all. She took his hand and lowered her voice.

'It's *safe*, honey! This is one of the only places in Europe where it's actually safe to paraglide, you know? You need the right wind conditions, obviously – the right winds to let you hover and swoop under your own control, but it's the take-off and landing that are tricky. Take-off in particular. You need the altitude to get right into the cut-and-thrust of the thermals, but you need a sort of runway, too – like a gradual slope to kick off until the wind gets underneath you. Most of the mountains round here are just peaks and rocks. You need the right slopes for a good take-off.'

Shaun nodded. 'Sounds bloody hit-and-miss if you ask me!'

'There's nothing to it! Not for you, anyway. Don't worry, handsome – I wouldn't drag you up here if I didn't absolutely know you'd love it. You told me you love being up on top of the mountains, yeah?'

He nodded again.

'Well, that's like . . . *nothing*! It's nothing. Wait till you've done this – it'll change your life!'

He gulped again. 'That's a bloody big kite you've got there.'

She gave him a reassuring look. 'That's what makes it safe. Come on. Hop in. Auntie Maggie's doing all the work today.'

He cheered a little. 'What? I don't have to go up on my own?'

'With no training? Don't talk shite!'

He started laughing fitfully, nervous but madly excited.

'No, we're going tandem. All you have to concentrate on is take-off and landing. When I've strapped us in right, and I pat you twice on the back, I want you to start running. All you have to remember to do is keep running. Even when you feel the tug of the wind, don't stop. Do not stop running until I tap you three times on the back.'

'Got you. What about landing?'

She threw him a helmet. 'I'll tell you all about that once we get up there. What we're going to do is fly over to the dam, about two or three miles east. I do that just with minimal little adjustments to the flight angle of the canopy. Then we're going to sweep right around to the coast, right over Nerja and Maro, and we're going to land on a little beach near San Cristobal. Same principle when we land. I tap you twice and you start pedalling those little legs like crazy. I'll talk you through it when it's time to land. Any questions?'

'Er, yeah – what about the car?'

She laughed. 'I send it down by parachute. No, I don't. There's a lad from Venta who drives it back down to the beach for me.'

Maggie stepped into her own sling, checked the tensile strength again and patted Shaun on his helmet. He grinned. He was gripped – terrified, but never in his life more desperate to go through with something.

'You OK?'

He nodded.

'Cool. Just relax. It might take a minute or two for the right breeze to come along. Might be a while. But as soon as I hit you, *run*, OK?'

'No problem. I can't wait.'

'Good lad. That's the way – be perfectly relaxed at all times. I'm a very experienced pilot. You're going to love it.'

They waited. For all her authority Shaun could sense Maggie's nervous anticipation as she stood dead still behind him, waiting for the moment. A sudden dread overtook him. What was he doing here? He was about to jump off a mountain with a complete stranger! He started trying to think of an acceptable order of words that'd get him out of it when he felt her tense behind him. Now she was picking something up, taking the strain and now, suddenly she was tapping him hard, twice. He couldn't move.

'GO!GO!GO!' she screamed, prodding him viciously

between the shoulder blades. 'MOVE IT! WE'RE GONNA LOSE THE BASTARD!'

Shaun managed to crank the funk out of his limbs and start a gentle jog down the slope. He found out why she hadn't wanted him to investigate the precipice any further. The calm scree ended abruptly about ten metres ahead of them, leaving only a short goat's trail and a seeming abyss beyond. It was a sheer drop.

Just then his legs lost their power. He was treading water on the spot, fighting against the current of the wind. A whiplash of sonic waves inside his ear and suddenly that enormous yellow canopy was flying up in front of them and now it was above and behind them, dragging them back, stopping them from running. He pushed on, got one foot in front of the other, using all his body strength to haul them onwards, then – WHOOSH! The wind caught and they were up, up in the sky.

Euphoria! His first thought was that nothing else anywhere in the world mattered. He wanted to scream for joy and jump out and just do it – sacrifice himself. The wind whipped the canopy, taking them higher again. The Vitara still looked close enough to spit on and Shaun could see now that that last ledge had not been sheer. There was a drop, then some bushes and a sandy footpath. But they would probably have broken a leg or so, if they'd carried on running and the canopy had failed to take. For a moment he just looked down, amazed as clouds appeared at his feet and the mountain peaks sat in silence below. He became aware of a tapping on his back, and a shrill sound. He twisted his head back to hear what she was telling him.

'You can stop running now!'

He looked down. His legs were still determinedly grinding away. He laughed, massively. He wanted to shout out. Down there was the soporific ocean, glass-flat apart from the white flume of the waves at the beachside. Even the microscopic boats and jet skis seemed stalled in that photographic still life. The hypnotic spectrum of the sea filtered out below, the translucid greens of the shallows dissolving into languid blues and the cold black chop of the depths far beyond.

The wind started to howl and whip the higher they climbed, making his ears ache. Tears streamed down his face, lashed by the sniping gusts, but still he wanted to go higher. He couldn't hear what Maggie was saying. He just nodded. They went higher. He could feel the tensile strength of the wires straining, humming in the high wind. He looked right up at the vast, confident parachute and held the stanchion tight.

The snowy peaks of the highest ranges were now frozen below them, tiny and precise. He was startled, overcome and totally unafraid. The Mercury Rev song 'Holes' came into his head. Serene and disembodied, it scored Shaun's sky-high feelings sublimely. Every few minutes the thought came to him that this whole structure, this sheet that was holding them up could fail, fail for a hundred reasons and send them crashing to extinction. He didn't care. From where he was now, nothing like that could have any meaning to him. This was just a wondrous flight.

They banked sharply and swooped downwards at speed, precipitating more slashing tears. He wiped his face and looked out at the sprawling lake. They were down below the peaks again now, with a more clement gale. The drill in his ears relented. For the first time the thought came to him that Hilary was down there, somewhere. She had no idea that that dot in the sky was her husband. Why should she?

They dropped away again, sweeping around towards the seaboard and, caught by a fast current at lower altitude, they now soared at speed over the surface of the ocean. Shaun held the stanchion for balance and twisted his face round to her.

'This is fantastic!'

He could hear her laughing, really laughing loud. She dropped the canopy slightly, letting the wind have its way with them. It tossed them from side to side in dramatic deep parabolas like the high boat-swing at the fairground, soaring so high that he thought they'd have to capsize, then plunging them back down and up again, high up to the other side. They levelled out and caught another strong gust, sailing fast and low. It was nirvana. He was full up. He wanted to tell her that he couldn't take any more when, as if sensing it, she tapped him twice and shouted: 'Pedal, boy!'

They swooped lower, able to hear the two-stroke engines of the motor boats now, and the gay chatter of the dozens on the beach. Shaun could make out individual features, sunglasses, bottles of Pepsi and 7-Up a hundred feet below but close enough to touch.

'Not so fast! We're coming in behind the beach, right? At the far end, where it's quite flat, see? Grass and sand.'

He nodded and gripped the steel structure again.

'It's easy. Relax. We want to take it at a very slow jog, going almost immediately into walking pace. Just get your first foot on the sand, jog, then walk. I'll do the rest.'

And she did. With such ease did Maggie bring the parachute down and fold it perfectly as it fell to the floor that Shaun felt quite acutely embarrassed by the fuss he'd made up there. But what an adventure! When he was sure she was finished and he wasn't burgling her attention, Shaun waded over to Maggie and hugged her. She was pleased, though she pretended to be blasé.

'So, what did I tell ya?'

'Everything,' grinned Shaun.

Pasternak felt not just cheerful – he was ecstatic! Having hatched his plan he couldn't wait to implement it, but they were well into siesta time, now. He'd have to seize his opportunity later. But he was certainly up to a little wander down to the beach, at any rate. He was more than up to it now. He spied the gang in their usual spot, more or less, and made his way over, still chuckling about his scheme.

It was the first traffic jam she'd known in Spain. She could see the problem – one-lane traffic up the hill and a convoy of oil tankers crawling up the incline at snail's pace. No one was going to risk overtaking on a hill – a slowly bending one at that with fast downhill traffic racing along the counterflow. She'd just have to sit it out until the dual carriageway, a mile or so away.

Her thoughts returned to Shaun. She'd been awful to him. She wouldn't blame him for the way he'd been that morning – she deserved it. But there was more to it. Callous though she'd been, her feeling was that Shaun would still not typically let himself react like that. Not that he'd *overreacted*, but he'd acted strongly. That was unlike him. It was unusual for him to be decisive when there was still the option of demurral. So, following that line, it was reasonable to assume that he wasn't acting in his own interests – which meant that he was doing this for her. He was trying to make it easy for her. Her understanding of it did not make her love him any better. Rather, he angered her again. Even her bravest bid for freedom was being produced and directed by him. She edged closer to the top of the hill, feeling suddenly and terribly alone. A single fat drop of rain burst on the windscreen.

Mikey was doodling in the sand with a charred, pointed stick, vaguely listening to Pasternak's crude sex jokes. Tom was in the sea. Everyone was groaning at the awful gags. To Mikey, it was too much. It was wrong.

'Fuck it! He turns up when he feels like it and gets everyone laughing straight away. He *has* to be centre of attention, the bastard! He deserves a bit of stick!' He raked an inquisitive look over his friend. 'Can you just explain that last one to me, Pastie?'

'How d'you mean?'

Mikey tried a humble expression and appealed round to the others, arms stretched out in pretend bewilderment. 'Well, I mean, I'm just a bit lost about the technicalities here. Why does he take it out after every thrust?'

Pasternak checked to make sure Mikey was kidding. 'Well – that's the joke, isn't it?'

'I know. But why's it funny? What's so funny about taking it right out and putting it back in again? Isn't that what people do?'

Pasternak began to redden. Only Mikey ever did this to him. What satisfaction did it give the bastard, roasting his friend like that? He tried to bluff it out. 'Don't be silly, Michael. I'm telling a joke. Please don't interrupt. You can go next.'

Mikey held up the flats of his palms, eyelids flickering madly. 'No. No. Stop.'

Pasternak rolled his eyes at the others.

'I want *you* to explain to *me*.'

'Explain what?'

'The facts of life.'

Pasternak laughed a high-pitched, squeaky laugh and reddened again. Individual, acorn-sized raindrops fell, one at a time, every half-minute or so, yet the sun blazed fiercely.

'Foolish boy!'

'No. You're not listening.' He prodded the sharp end of the stick at Pasternak. 'I want *you* to tell me, how *you* do it. How do *you* prefer to lubricate a woman? What's *your* insertion technique? Hmm? Hmm? You can't answer, can you?'

Anke hit him over the arm. 'Mikey? Stop!'

He turned to her. 'He can't answer because . . .'

Millie, who had been suffering with every shade of Pasternak's exposure and embarrassment, interrupted. 'Because he's a real man. Sure, he makes the vulgar jokes but he's far too sensitive to embarrass me in front of you guys.'

Mikey spluttered. His eyes shot from Millie to Pasternak back to Millie. 'You and Pastie?'

She rolled her eyes. 'All the time. Whenever we can find somewhere.' She leaned over to Mikey and whispered loud enough for everyone to hear. 'And let me tell you, Mikey, baby – us girls like to talk as well, you know. And I think I know who got the better man!'

Mikey glared wildly from Anke to Millie to Pasternak.

Pasternak didn't laugh or crow or make anything of it. He just wanted an end to it, now. Mikey looked him in the eye. He managed a humble grimace and a nod of confirmation. Mikey looked gutted. He hurled his stick at the nearest palm tree.

'I don't believe you! He's a fucking virgin!'

Everyone looked at the floor, the trees, the sea.

'Anyone fancy a beer?' wondered Pasternak.

Maggie returned from the beach bar carrying two beers.

'That's everything packed away safe and sound. Lot of messing about for an hour in the sky, hey?'

'Oh, but worth it! I mean, that was just . . .' He tailed off, shaking his head. He looked up and down the small, secluded beach. A few camper vans were parked up together over by the bamboo-fringed bar. Closer to the water's edge, groups of young surfers and beach bums sat around smoking and laughing.

'This is perfect. Thanks.'

She gave his shoulder a squeeze. 'I'm glad you're happy.'

He turned to smile at her, squinting against the sun. 'I am. That's the main thing about being up there, you know?'

She shrugged and took a swig of her beer, inviting him to continue.

'I could just see the whole picture. It was like – everything has its place. Do you know what I mean?'

She nodded and smiled. 'No.'

'I mean, like – I've always been able to sense all that. I've always had a good sense of, you know, nature's *balance* if you like. That's why I still feel so sorry for Hilary. I mean – she's denied me sex for over two years. But I sort of agree with her. I understand.'

Maggie jerked her bottle out of her mouth, half choking. 'Whoa! Hold it, man! One thing at a time . . . One minute we're up in the sky, in harmony with the world and God's great bountiful nature . . .' She leaned forward to him and took hold of both wrists. '*How* long?'

He released himself and took a drink, trying to emphasise that this was serious stuff. 'Look. I *know*. It's brutal. It's grounds for any number of atrocities. Divorce, at least. Or adultery. But . . . ah, fuck! It's hard to explain.' He turned right round to let her know that this was the good bit. 'I've never seen the point of attrition. I think you've just got to try and see things for what they are and make your decisions accordingly. And with Hils, like – for all that it was all against me, you know, I could kind of understand it. I could get the sense of how, sort of, *lost* she was. But she doesn't even want that. She doesn't want understanding. She just wants to get on with it on her own now, I think.'

Maggie watched him with increasing empathy and, once he'd finished talking, she leaned across and gave his hand the slightest squeeze. They both sipped at their bottles. Maggie snatched a sideways look at him and stifled a smile, swigging at her drink as though she was trying to spit her grin into the beer. The express of her breath made a disembodied hum on the mouth of the bottle. It was hopeless. A surging wave of hilarity came over her. She cackled out loud and pounced on him.

'Two years! You poor sod! You must be going up the wall!'

He threw her off, smiling. 'I've had some disturbing thoughts, yes!'

She pinned him down. 'I'm going to spirit you away and jump your bones! No back answers!'

He wrestled her over so that he was on top, dragged the sandy hair from his eyes and tucked it behind his ear. Droplets of rain big enough to catch plopped all around them, one at a time, exploding and refracting the splintered sunlight.

'We'll just have to see.'

'Minge teaser!'

He looked down at her, trying to do a Parker voice. 'That is not the language of a refined Dunbar college gel what has qualifications and certificates, m'lady.'

The surfers' parasol buckled under a sudden gust, strained to hold its position then flew clear of its mooring. It spun in the air for a second then crashed back to the ground again, running away down the beach like tumbleweed. The surfers gave chase, eventually having to dive and grab it before it hit the sea. A rainbow cut the sky, still bright and blue-hot above the beach, but low and heavy over the mountains. Another squall whipped up towels and beach mats. Some of the beach kids started to retreat to their Dormobiles. Maggie got up, too.

'Come on. I've left the roof off the car. This is going to blow up in a minute.'

'Let's stay! It's exciting!'

'Believe me, there's nothing too exciting about sand in your mouth, sand in your eyes, sand in your ears. Unless you like sand.' She looked around her. Everyone was dragging up their belongings and making a run for it. 'Look. Even the bar's closing down for the day. This could be a biggie.'

'A biggie? You don't have biggies in Spain!'

She hauled him to his feet. 'Oh, we do. Not so often, mind, but when the mistral hits, she hits!'

'Wow!'

He took a last look up at the darkening sky and ran after her.

After Pasternak went off on his secret mission, assuring them he needed neither help nor company, everyone split and went their own way. Matt asked Millie if she fancied staying on the beach but she winced at the stiffening breeze. She said she needed to go into Nerja to buy a few presents anyway. Her invitation for Matt to join her wasn't even half-hearted. He guessed she was going to try and find Pastie.

Matt set off back up the steps, thinking he'd doze by the pool, do a few laps, whatever. Just as he had done every day since they'd got there, he started off trying to count the number of steps up to the resort – someone had told him a hundred and sixty-nine – but as always, he stopped halfway up to look back at the beach and watch the goldfish swimming by the waterfall. A lizard, wide and pale and flat as though it had been squashed underfoot, froze on the wall by his hand. He didn't move. The lizard watched him, rock still. Matt got bored waiting for it to scurry away and pushed himself off from the lip of wall. By the time he started into the final haul, through the jungle of pungent white and pink orchids, nodding in the wind like flagrant bells, he'd forgotten where he was up to. He was sure it was more than a hundred and sixty-nine. It felt more like five hundred in this humidity, even with the occasional gust.

He stopped at the top to catch his breath. Stifling and squalid, the atmosphere felt ready to burst. The rising amphitheatre of apartments and villas seemed to have trapped the heat in a vacuum, with no respite for those who had to venture through it. The terracotta tiles were scalding. The air was slick and muggy with the threat of rain. He could think no further than getting himself to the pool and hurling himself into its chlorine chill.

He didn't see her at first. He dived in, swam, showered, laid down his towel and started to drowse in the sunshine, thinking that the holiday had been fine, good fun, but that he should maybe also make some new friends when he got back home. Home. The very word, even as a spoken concept inside his head, summoned up memories of the orphanage. He screwed up his eyes to get himself back to now. Friends. He loved Pastie. Tom and Mikey were all right. He needed some variety, though. Perhaps they were all just a little bit childish.

He propped his chin up and looked around the pool area. He would have missed her again, hidden away over by the big fat yucca tree, had she not sat up just then and started applying cream to her shoulders. Matt smiled, woozily happy to see her, and gathered up his things to join her.

'You've missed a bit,' he grinned.

She was surprised at how pleased she was to see him. She hadn't spoken to anyone since Shaun walked out that morning. Matt squatted down.

'Shall I do that?'

She gave him a warning look. 'Of course. I forgot it was your speciality.'

It took him a moment to twig.

'She's my mate's girlfriend. Well, sort of – they met out here.'

'Looked like you're all on quite intimate terms.'

'We ARE!' He was flustered. 'We get on. He was just being an arsehole. He wouldn't do her back for her. It just seemed, sort of, nasty of him, you know?'

She decided not to rib him further. And she felt curiously liberated by his version of events, too. She handed him the bottle, looking him right in the eye.

'Go on. Let's see what you're made of. Give me a really good going over.'

She couldn't believe she'd said that! She turned her face away from him so that she could smile to herself. She uncoiled herself, preparing for the first touch. Nothing happened. A knee came into her field of vision. My God! He was straddling her!

She closed her eyes, happy just to let things be. She breathed in the sweet, cloying coconut as a slow trail of lotion rippled down her spine. He left it to drip ticklishly as he replaced the lid and put the bottle back on the ground. She could feel the silky cream running down her sides, trickling towards her bottom. She tensed her buttocks, waiting for the unctuous slither of the lotion but, just as it was about to hit, there was the gentle press of his thumbs at the base of her spine. He caught the cream in a chevron, two thumbs joined at their tips and, like a pinball wizard, propelled it back, smoothing a strong pressure back along the furrow of muscle, coaxing her to relax and yield. Once her back was covered with a thin sheen, he started again at the small of her back, walking his fingers along her spine, delicately circling each vertebra with precise motifs then moving up to the next, unpicking her tension, her fear, her cares.

She let out a long sigh and gave in completely. Feeling her succumb, Matt softened the impact and the intensity, using the subtlety of his fingertips to ply and strum the delicate skin on her ribcage. She slumped under his manipulation, perfectly supple and willing now. He kneaded her shoulders, exerting his thumbs to pop and smooth out little knots of stress. With three fingers of each hand he circled the sides of her neck and throat, making her bite hard to stifle a moan.

'Hilary,' he said softly, not wanting to invade her drowsy, drifting state. 'I need you to take your top right off.'

She didn't even question it. She nodded minutely, straightening her arms to slide her bikini top away.

'That's better. Now I can really work on these last few areas . . . of . . . resistance . . .'

With each word he dug hard into the base of her back and, flattening his hands out and using his whole body, eased the firm balls of his palms slowly, slowly up her back. She could feel his cock gouging into her backside as he pushed, caressed and retreated. She gripped a tuft of grass, trying to fight it, sure she was going to give herself away. The sensation, the release, the freedom - it was too much for her, too good to be true. If he'd slipped a hand, a finger, between her legs she would have let him carry on. She would have parted, just a little, enough for him to find her. She was losing it. He must be able to smell her, surely. She craned her head and tried to find a voice.

'Matt. That was just . . . wonderful. I'm really thirsty. Would you like a drink?'

'Sure. Shall I go?'

He jumped off. She sat up and reached for her top. His eyes were fleetingly all over her little tits at the same time as she cased his knob. Definitely a semi, if not the full boner. She hooked herself up, feeling strange, stranger than she could ever recall.

Having come all that way, Pasternak was determined not to go back empty-handed. Bloody siesta! If *his* shops took a siesta he'd be down about twenty-five per cent! That's how much lunchtime business was worth to the diligent storekeeper. He'd just have to wait until four and hope that, after all that, they had what he was looking for. Then it was just a case of locating tablets. Easy, surely in a town this size – a tourist town, above all.

The rain finally came, and in deluges, driving the sun-worshippers from the poolside. Hilary and Matt, under the shelter of the bar's woven grass roof, hardly noticed. Hilary was listening intently to Matt, staring straight ahead at the pool as he told of his early life in a North Wales orphanage. She should have guessed it was something like that, with him.

'I mean, it was quite nice, sort of. I was happy. It's what you know, isn't it? Some of the older women in the home, the religious ones, like – they tried to upset us. Once I stole a jar of jam from the kitchen – not just for me like, everyone had it – but she made me confess and, like, in front of everyone she battered me with a stick and said we shouldn't expect anything different from the son of a prostitute. I didn't know what she was talking about.'

Hilary wanted to go to him, to stroke his hair but he made no eye contact. He carried on staring into the pool's rainy ripples.

'Things like that stick out in your memory, but I don't think it bothered me too much. The orphanage was fine. I've got a lot to thank them for. And I found out what love is.'

Now he looked at her. He seemed to be asking permission to continue. She touched his hand.

'What happened?'

He forced a laugh. 'I still don't really know.' He shook his head, faraway eyes searching for a clue. He took a gulp of his Coke.

'She worked in the kitchens at first, Amanda – that's when I first saw her. I was about ten or eleven, cheeky little get, I suppose, and she always used to smile at me and give me a little bit more. She went away but she came back a year or two later, as a live-in.'

'What's that?'

'Oh – sort of a teacher, but they do everything.'

'Like house parents?'

'I suppose, but Amanda – she was only a kid herself. It was awful, worse for her, I suppose. We knew what we were doing was supposed to be wrong. But it wasn't. We loved each other. It was the most beautiful time. The best thing I've ever known.'

'What happened? To her?'

'Wish I knew. I heard stories, but you never know what to believe in a place like that. The only facts, right . . .' His face strained as he was talking. 'I've thought about this, over and over – but all I'm left with is that she disappeared. Upped and went. Jimmy Clowes, my best mate back there and I don't see why he'd lie – he said there was a terrible argument, real bad shouting from the live-in quarters. Dame Slap – she's the one who said about me mother – he could hear her screaming and Amanda crying. But you never knew with Jimmy. He was in a world of his own, most of the time. I mean, *I* never heard nothing.'

She stroked his hand again. 'If you take a step back from it, though – it does have a logic, doesn't it? How old was she?'

He shrugged. 'Twenty?'

'So a twenty-year-old woman, yes, an adult and whether you like it or not a woman in a position of trust . . .'

'She wasn't! She was . . . Amanda!'

She hesitated. 'But Matt, to the authorities, to the board of governors she was breaching basic fundamental trust.' She leaned towards him to make him understand. 'It was cardinal sin! If they knew she was having a sexual relationship with one of her charges, a *boy*, for God's sake!'

'I was fourteen. I was a man!'

'Not to your guardians. She *had* to go.'

'Without saying goodbye? Without a note?'

'The people at the orphanage?'

He nodded.

'They'd have insisted upon a complete severance of contact. They probably wanted to turn her over to the police – strictly speaking, they should have done. Perhaps they wanted to spare you.'

'They never made any reference to it!'

Hilary watched the rain strafe the pool's surface. She

sighed and tried to make him look at her. 'You've just got to accept that! That's often how people deal with things they don't like. They just brush them away, hide them out of sight!'

Now he flashed her a look. 'Is that what you've done with your fella?'

She held his look, then smiled. 'I'm not sure.'

Matt sighed out loud and toppled his chair on to its back legs. 'No. No one is. No one knows anything, do they?'

The rain seemed softer. The sun was breaking through in shafts. She got up and laid her hand on his head, stroking his troubled temple with her thumb.

'I don't suppose they do, Matt.' She fiddled with the neck of her bottle, not sure what she wanted to say. 'Thanks for keeping me company. I'd better go.'

She kissed him on the cheek and hurried away, hunched against the rain. Matt watched her go. He liked her. He really liked her. He hadn't meant to come on heavy like that. He fished the slice of lemon out of his Coke, still rocking his chair back and forward. He sucked on the sharp spike of lemon. The bar owner came to collect their glasses, reminding Matt he was the only person left at the pool.

He got up to go. As he pushed the chair back with his calves, he spotted her canvas duffel bag under the table. Shit! He didn't even know which apartment she was in. He knew she usually came and went from the back gate, but he had only a vague idea after that. He snatched up the bag and ran out into the rain. It was delicious, warm and probing as it speared his scalp and neck. He bounded down the steps, two and three at a time and followed his instincts, taking the left fork. He ran quickly, looking right and left and, as he got to the top of a steep flight leading to the lake one way, and more apartments straight ahead, he saw her right down at the bottom. He was about to shout to her but she was still some distance away. Running sideways on he hurried down, catching sight of her at the moment she got to her door and threw her head back in dismay, realising she'd left her bag all the way back at the bar. He loped up behind her, slowing now to catch his breath.

'Looking for this?' he gasped, grinning, crouching to rest his palms on his thighs.

She made big eyes at him and took the bag, fishing out her keys. She unlocked the door, her throat and her stomach tightening. She stood in the doorway, unsure, not turning round. Matt came up behind her and held her arms just below her shoulders. She reached behind her and touched his thigh, pulling her fingers away again immediately. He moved his hands up to her shoulders, still moist with raindrops. He stooped to suck the droplets from the hollow of her collarbone. Her neck tingled.

'Come in and close the door.'

Still she stood with her back to him. She shivered slightly. He put his arms right around her and bent to kiss her nape. She backed into him.

'Matt . . .'

He cupped her breasts roughly through the sodden bikini, kissing her neck and the side of her face, on fire now, grinding into her backside. She seemed to tense and fight herself then, shoulders relenting, she breathed out, long and slow, and went slack. She nestled her bottom into him and rubbed back against his cock.

'This is . . .'

She turned around to see him. He was beautiful, eager, waiting. She held his lovely face in her hands. He backed her towards the wall and pinned her there. She spread out her arms, eyes questioning him. He put his hands over hers and leaned into her and this time she kissed him with all her heart, all her anger and love and frustration rising up as she threw herself into the embrace, biting his lips, seeking his tongue and his dick. He pulled away from her, breathless, and looked into her face.

'Jesus, Hilary!' he panted.

Hilary closed her eyes.

'You've got to let me! Let me fuck you!'

She inclined her head, once. Yes.

Shaun, cosy in the enveloping wrap of the big beach towel, sipped his chocolate, knowing he'd have to show his hand soon. Maggie came back from the bedroom, still drying her hair, a smaller towel tucked under her armpits.

'Some downpour!'

'Beauty, wasn't it?'

They sat in silence. She sat with her back propped against the sofa, one leg crooked to rest her mug on, the other stretched out straight. She even had freckles on her shiny shins. She smiled naughtily but carried on looking into her cup.

'Two years?'

Shaun shifted position. 'Look. I mentioned that for a reason, and only in a certain context.'

'Touchy!'

'Not really.'

She took a sip and curved her lips at him. She was very attractive. He would love to kiss her.

'And what was the context?'

'About being up there, like a bird. It's going to sound silly now.'

'No – it won't. I'm sorry.'

He paused to think it out. 'I don't know. Just a general understanding that things are what they are. I could have begged and sulked and *got* sex. Or I could easily have gone to another woman. But what would that have been?'

She shrugged. 'A shag?'

He closed his eyes. When he opened them she was coming over to him. She took his mug from his hand and kissed him lightly, then leaned back for his reaction. He hung his head.

'Would you think me a terrible crank if I asked if we could just go to bed and hold each other?'

'I certainly would. And I can think of nothing I'd like more than to go to bed and just hold you and have you hold me.'

'Really?'

She nodded.

'I think I'm going to fall in love with you.'

'God help you.'

Not to put too fine a point on it, Pasternak was twatted. The guy he'd been put on to by the DJ in Club Torro had seemed more enthusiastic about sampling his own wares than taking any money for them. He'd shown Pasternak Mitsubishis, Lips, Euros, Apples and e-mails, popping one of each into his mouth and actually chewing them, rather than necking them with a drink.

He showed no eagerness to sell and no inclination to offer Pastie any, either. Finally he came to the point. He produced a little bag of 125s and held them up like a conjuror, eyes wide as though he was about to make them disappear again. But he didn't. He indicated for Pasternak to put his tongue out, placed a tablet on his tongue and watched eagerly while he swallowed. He carried on watching.

'Eh? Eh?' he leered, nodding at Pasternak, who nodded back, trying to convey the appropriate amount of out-of-it-ness with his eyes.

'Mmm,' he said, making a circle with his thumb and forefinger.

'Is good? Is good?' growled the founder of the feast.

'Is a bit bloody early to say,' thought Pasternak, nodding madly.

The dealer pulled out a sachet. He looked like a deranged pirate with his single hoop earring and his four-day stubble. He was Alexei Sayle with hair.

'How many you want?'

Pasternak tried to look modest. 'Oh – six, *por favor*.'

Alexei's swarthy face went grey. 'Six? Six? Don't you waste my fuckin' time with six! Ramon say you crazy boy! Say you want drog!'

'I do!'

'Six!'

Pasternak tried to recall how much money he had on him. He held out a hand to calm the angry pirate, who'd subtly shifted from Jolly Roger to Captain Hook in the blink of an eye. Or the flicker of an eye, in his case – while one sticky eyelid stayed almost shut throughout the transaction, the other blinked feverishly at Pasternak.

'Seven, then. I'll take seven.'

The dealer batted a hand at Pasternak, stood up and went to walk away. 'Don't waste my time! Move.'

Pasternak didn't know what to do. He really needed the Es. The plan was redundant without them.

'I'll have eight. Eight of those last ones.'

'The 125?' He looked away and spoke to the road, jolting his leg nervously. 'Minimum twelve.'

'What?'

He flashed the briefest of looks back at Pasternak. 'Big demand for 125. Twelve is minimum order.'

Fuck! Pasternak tried to work out how much twelve tablets'd cost. Say they were twenty quid each, say £250 for the twenty, that's . . . about 60,000. Sixty mil! He had about 45,000 on him. He tried not to sound ruffled.

'Twelve, hey? Twelve minimum.' He plopped his bottom lip out, shrugged and did a little boxer's shimmy, like he was trying to work something out. 'OK. What's twelve weigh in at?'

'Excuse?'

'How much?'

The pirate was best friends again. He gave Pasternak a careful look. 'Thirty mil.'

The relief coasted through him. Hallelujah! He was saved! His Big Last Night could go ahead as planned. But there was still the fun of the deal to be concluded. The pirate's look had given everything away. He didn't expect to get anything like thirty mil for his tablets.

'I've got fifteen.'

'I need thirty.'

He was talking over his shoulder to the road again. Pasternak sipped his beer.

'Well . . . I can give you ten now and take six pills,

then I'll come back tomorrow and give you another ten.'

The pirate was bamboozled. Pasternak knew he wouldn't want to come back. He had plenty of stock. His game was to get as much hard cash in his pocket as possible, right here, right now.

'You got fifteen mil?'

Pasternak nodded. The pirate took a couple of tablets out of the sachet.

'For this I give you ten, yes? You lucky I have a good day today.'

Pasternak shrugged his acquiescence.

'Fifteen mil.'

Pasternak, deft as ever when it came to handling money, separated three 5,000 notes in his pocket and whipped them out. The pirate shook hands, took the money and was gone. Pasternak inspected the pills, half expecting a switch or a light order, but everything seemed fine. He thought he might as well drop another one, just for the hell of it, just in case he ran into Millie on the way home.

Mistake. If the first one would have set off a kaleidoscope of sherbet fountains and a gradually heightening sexual impulse, the second depth charge triggered a minefield of unchecked lust. Pasternak wandered back up the coast road to the resort, mindless of time or place, stopping every group of females he passed to ask for sex. By the law of averages he should, sooner or later, have stumbled upon the sort of girls Matt encountered on the first night although it's not certain that even they would have responded to his duck call.

'Hey! You! Come over here and let me give you one! Come on! Anyone can see you're gagging for it!'

He stumbled on into the night, something in the dim recesses of his psyche telling him it would all be fine tomorrow. Tomorrow was going to be The Day.

For a long time they just sat there, arms around each other, letting the waves wash over their feet. The faint flamenco of the beach bars and tourist cafés drifted into the still night. Matt looked up at the bright Mediterranean night sky.

'Look at the stars!'

'Beautiful.'

He pulled her closer. 'Are you OK?'

She kissed him. 'I'm . . .' She shrugged. 'I couldn't be happier.'

'Not feeling bad about it?'

'No. Not a bit. It was perfect.'

'Good.'

He picked up a pebble and tossed it into the sea. 'What happens now?'

'Don't know.'

'What d'you want to happen now?'

'For tonight to go on and on, and for me not to have to think about tomorrow.'

'So you *do* feel guilty.'

'No. It's different. Not guilty, no. It wasn't dirty.' She took his hand. 'Just a little sorry for him. He's one of the good ones. It's hard.'

Matt threw another stone. 'Maybe he feels the same?'

'Maybe. I'm not looking forward to seeing him, though.'

'No.'

She took him by surprise, pinning him down and covering his face in kisses. 'Nothing, though – nothing is going to make me feel bad about today!'

He pulled her close into him, relishing the slim dip of her waist against his trailing fingertips. 'So we could see each other again?'

She kissed him longingly, sliding her tongue behind his teeth, all the time holding his face in her hands. She stood up, watching him carefully. 'I'd better go. I'll find you tomorrow.'

He looked down, reaching for more pebbles. 'You won't, though, will you?'

She knelt down again, anxious. 'Why are you saying that, Matt?'

He shrugged. 'Just a feeling. Just the way it goes, I suppose.'

She kissed the top of his head. 'I'll come and find you tomorrow.'

She walked back from the beach to the lights of the bars and restaurants, stopped once to look back at her lover, see if he was waving. He looked desolate. Back hunched, all alone, he threw stone after stone into the surf. He seemed already to have made up his mind that this was the end, already. She started up the steps. She was on a high. She didn't know what to think.

Day Seven

She choked off the alarm so as not to wake Shaun, but he still wasn't back. When she'd let herself into the apartment last night, ready to sit down with him, utterly unsure what she'd say, she was relieved at his absence, glad of the reprieve. At that point she could only imagine he'd been up in the sierras, or mooching around an ancient settlement somewhere. She was sure he'd be back at any moment, and quickly got herself off to bed with a vague notion of the moral advantage it would give her to be asleep when he got back.

But Shaun did not come back. Strangely bereft, she set herself to washing and dressing loosely for t'ai chi. Her thoughts fluctuated between Matt and Shaun, giving every stage of her routine – each cleansing buff of the cotton-wool ball, each precise stroke of the sun block – extra significance. She felt like a harlot, tearing both men apart carelessly. She quite liked the idea.

Where *was* he, though? Where was Shaun? She felt a sudden spurt of anxiety. Perhaps he had been involved in an accident and the police were even now trying to track her down? She remembered that icy morning his foreman had called to inform her about his fall. She got to imagining a fully developed scenario involving Shaun's lonely death at the roadside. He was hitchhiking along the busy coast road. It was twilight, turning to dark. The lorry driver was half drunk. Shaun didn't know a thing about it. She went off into conspicuous detail, wondering whether Shaun carried ID with him, trying to work out how long it would take for the authorities to identify him and trace her and come and knock at the door and break the tragic news. It could take days. She imagined herself running to Matt for comfort. He would suggest that she shouldn't be on her own at a time like this. They'd be together.

She came out of the reverie, found herself looking at her image in the mirror, toothbrush in hand, stuck in a trance. She laughed, half disgusted with herself for thinking like that. But she was thinking it – that was the thing.

She jogged lightly to the pool, enjoying the cool light of the early morning, the abundant and fragrant flora, the slow, gradual infusion of the day. There was no escaping it. She felt *good*. She felt like she was on the verge of something. Optimism, anticipation, thrilling, placeless excitement, *power* – these were the surges and eddies she tried to ignore as she started into her warm-up. But it was hopeless. She could not filter out snatches of reminiscence, thoughts of big things just around the corner. The state of serenity she needed for a fulfilling yang was never going to be hers today. Hilary stopped still and looked up to the hills, hands on her hips, full of courage. She was ready.

Pasternak was dying for a drink. He started to think that the dryness of his aching bones would cut right through his skin if he didn't water himself soon. His skull seemed to expand and retract with each stab of breath, but still he couldn't make himself get up for a drink. He remembered the tablets and smiled to himself. If he could just get himself back to sleep now, he'd be in tremendous shape for the Big One.

Hilary was overjoyed to hear his key in the lock. It was a complex sensation, part joyful relief that he was fine, but there was excitement, too, a nervous enlightenment she knew she could share with him. She was about to run and hug him, but just in time grasped back an image of how inappropriate that might be. It would have been tantamount to her rushing over and trilling: 'Darling! I've decided I'm definitely leaving you! But it's best for you, too! Isn't it just wonderful?'

So she waited for him to come through the door, and the two of them stood there and looked at each other despondently, knowing everything – and then Shaun just came across and smothered her with his broad arms.

'Oh, Hilary! Hilary, Hilary, Hilary.'

She tiptoed up to him and kissed him on the cheek.

'Cup of tea?'

'Fantastic.'

'Sit down.'

She poked her head through the hatch, worried.

He smiled up at her.

'I'm fine.'

She brought the teas through, careful now not to upset the goodwill between them. She sipped at the steam of it, her lips retreating from the scalding surface of the drink. She set her cup down.

'Shaun?'

'Mmm?'

'If . . .'

She stopped and looked away, her eyes suddenly filling up. Shaun put his drink down and took her hand.

'Go on.'

She took a breath. 'If we both feel the same about this . . .' She looked up for reassurance. 'If we think, maybe, that it's probably best . . .'

He nodded, looking at the floor.

'Then, you know, given all that – it might be best not to have the big break-up conversation, if you know what I mean. Do you see what I'm saying?'

He nodded again. 'Think so.'

'It could only lead to us saying bad things. Things we might not even . . .'

He shushed her. He reached for her tea, passed it to her, reached for his own.

'No. I do, I think I know what you mean. It's like, quit while you're ahead, sort of, isn't it?'

She nodded and sipped her tea. He looked at his, absent-mindedly picking at a stray tea leaf.

'There's one thing, though. Just from a practical point of view. I mean, I was thinking – I've really found something out here, these last few days. It's hard to explain all the things that have happened. I saw an eagle, you know!'

She smiled. Same thing. She wanted to share his childish excitement, but she found herself annoyed, instead.

'I just think that, if it's feasible, I wouldn't mind staying on a few days. Depends on flights and all that, of course.'

'Where will you stay?'

He wafted his hand at the problem. 'Ah, there's *pensións* in town, dead cheap. I'd hardly need any money. All I seem to eat is bread and olives. Big bottle of water. That's all you need. There's no charge for the mountains and the sea.'

She could sense that familiar frustrated, blunted anger coming back. Nothing would be gained by giving vent to it, but this was *so* Shaun! A major life-change happens, a turn of events that most would find traumatic. How does her husband deal with it? No problem. Off you go, ex-wife! I'll just give myself another week's holiday. She couldn't stop herself.

'D'you think that's fair?'

'How is it not fair?'

'Well, you know . . .' She forced a laugh. 'I mean, we'd all like an extra few days in the sun . . .'

'And?'

'Some of us have to go back to work.'

'Some of us don't.'

Détente was over.

'Oh, fuck off! You're impossible!'

'Why?'

She strove for the right answer. She came up with the wrong one.

'Who's going to pay for this little consolation prize, anyway?'

'I wondered when we'd get down to that.'

'Well, don't just wonder! Confront it! Change of flight ticket, yes? Accommodation? Food and drink?'

She floundered for more examples.

'Taxi to airport, telephone calls. Have you thought about any of this? You're talking two hundred quid or more! When were you going to get around to asking me for it?'

'Have I asked you for anything?'

She snorted dismissively, demeaning him. It had simply not entered her head that Shaun could have lined up his own gig. He looked at her, so waspish, so bristling, so needing a short sharp shock. He wanted to say it. He knew he shouldn't, but he wanted to say it. He *wanted* to say it. Shit. It was coming out.

'How do you know I haven't met a lovely local girl who works for an airline who would gladly put me up, feed me and swap my flight ticket for the cost of an administration fee?'

Hilary was agog. Thinking about it later there were many things she could have said, but what she came out with was: 'Have you?'

Shaun looked away.

'Have you slept with her?'

He didn't answer.

She spoke quietly. 'You bastard.'

'I'm not.'

She mustered up all the contempt she could raise. 'A little Spanish air hostess! How sweet! And did she do everything you wanted? Was she good?' Her eyes were full of tears. 'Hope she's got a nice moustache!'

Shaun got to his feet. 'I don't get you! This is madness! You've got what you want. I'm not crawling at your feet begging for another chance. I've come round to your way of thinking. I'm out. What's the problem?'

She looked forlorn. She slumped down in the chair, hugging a cushion to her. 'I don't know. I wish I knew.'

He offered his hand and pulled her up and held her. She snuffled on his chest. He softened his voice, sorry he'd said it, wanting to reassure her.

'Look. I haven't slept with anyone. I would have thought you knew me better. I haven't and I wouldn't. I'm just – whatever's happened to us, right, it's happened. You were dead right. You could see it for

what it was. You owned up to it first and, you know –
that was *so* brave. People just don't have the guts to do
that – certainly not on holiday! But we've got to see it
through now.' He made her look at him. 'Haven't we?'

She nodded.

'I don't know about you, but I've started to feel all
right about it. I've been sitting round, on buses,
whatever, and all I can see is people who are miserable.
Just sticking it out, you know?'

'I know.'

'And, last few days I've just been thinking.'

He started nodding enthusiastically. 'Yeah. Nice one,
Hilary. Cruel but honest sort of thing.'

'You always were a sentimental bastard!'

'No, but really. I mean . . .' He struggled for the right
way of expressing himself. 'Maybe people just run out
of steam, hey? Maybe we're not *meant* to stay together.

She smiled, a faraway look in her moist eyes. 'It *is*
crazy though, isn't it? You think of the girls at school
who marry their first boyfriend. Madness! Even if
you've been out with fifty boys, who's to say you
should live your life with one of them? There might be
someone nicer in Guatemala!'

'Wheel of fortune . . .'

'Russian fucking roulette, more like!'

'So.' He pecked her on the forehead. 'We haven't
done so bad, with our little contribution, have we?'

'No. It was nice to start with.'

He picked up his cup and clinked with hers.

'To the way we were.'

'Yes. The way we were.'

They both sipped at their tea, eyes down.

★

Hilary had asked Shaun if he wanted to walk into Nerja with her and he'd said yes, but just as quickly he changed his mind, told her he'd prefer to just see it out on his own. They were both choked. They sat there, unsure what else to say, until Hilary smiled sadly at him and got up to go out.

Shaun kicked around the flat for a while, trying to put a plan together. In twenty-four hours she would be gone. He wasn't taking that flight tomorrow – Maggie or not, Shaun was determined to stay on in Nerja for as long as it felt right, or as long as he could. The details were cloudy but his resolve and the impulse underpinning it was strong. Until Hilary had gone, he could only consider that it was best for them to keep apart. Whatever was going to happen, it would happen fully, in the fullness of time.

He decided to walk down to the beach. He'd hardly been down there and, from the look of the detailed local map he picked up at the caves, there was a clifftop trail he could follow from the beach up and across to Maro. Maybe Maggie would be back from work by the time he idled over there. If not, he could leave a note.

Vaulting down the steps with renewed purpose and a gladdening heart, Shaun was stopped in his tracks by a woman in a bright red suit, arm extended like a policeman halting traffic. She was gurning in a baroque, yet triumphant manner. It was Davina from Sunflight.

'Ha! Gotcha! Who's been a naughty boy?'

How can she possibly know, thought Shaun. Unless she was a colleague of Maggie's? Perhaps he and Hilary had become a staple on the travel rep gossip grapevine.

'Who didn't attend any of my little get-togethers?'

Her fingers were up, describing her inverted commas for his delectation. Shaun blinked at her.

'I'm sorry . . .'

'Oh, don't worry yourself! It's not what we tend to think of as compulsory. Some clients are great believers in what I like to call freelancing it. Dee aye why!'

Shaun mugged up for her, wondering what the heck this was about. The sun was at its height, directly above the centre of his skull and beating, beating, beating down hard on him. He was starting to wilt. He'd have to move on, or get himself into the shade, anything. He was starting to gasp.

'What, er . . .' he croaked, unable to finish the sentence. He was expiring quickly.

She fished into her bag. 'I was just on my way up to yours. Just wanted to pop this under the door . . .'

He watched her mouth closely as she said 'dorrrr'. It seemed to move independently of the rest of her face and regardless of the sense of her words. Shaun continued gaping at her, waiting for a clue. He realised he was staring solely at her mouth, subconsciously refining his attention to the source of news, enlighten-ment and, soon he prayed, freedom.

'Is everything OK, my ducks?'

'Fine. Excellent.'

She was still waving a leaflet at him, waiting for him to take it. 'It's just pick-up arrangements for tomorrow.' She hunched up her shoulders, looking like a Krankie. 'Unless you're planning to stow away here and, how shall we say, abscond?'

He looked at her blankly. If she didn't fuck off in the next minute he was going to collapse right there, at her feet. She beamed brightly at him.

'Well! You've saved me a journey up all them steps, thank you very much! Do us a favour, though, hon? Have a peep at the return home details. What I do try to say about the times is . . .' More inverted commas. ' "Be early." Don't give them that excuse. They do tend to be what I like to call "temperamental", time-wise. Ciao!'

She shrunk her head into her shoulders again, grinned and vanished. Shaun staggered back under a tree and sat there, gasping and fanning himself. The prospect of an ice-cold Cruzcampo and a paddle in the sea had never seemed so appealing.

Matt was waiting by the pool when she got back from Nerja. Seeing his face light up with pleasure as she pushed open the wrought-iron gate instantly filled her with pity. She was sorry for his naivety, sorry for his vulnerability, sorry for her prior glimpse at the way it would inevitably be. But all of that came as a fleeting and spasmodic sense. There was nothing more to it than a gentle and general tristesse, and it was gone as soon as it came. She was sad to see how openly, how hugely besotted he was, how much of himself he was ready to give. But she could be the same. She didn't want to demonstrate it to everybody around the pool but she knew it was true – she was overjoyed to see him there. She wanted to be with him. She did. She dropped her bags by his towel. He sat up.

'I've been counting the hours.'

'Me too.'

'I wanted to come and watch you this morning. I tried to stay awake.' He rolled his eyes. 'Pastie was on one again.'

'The philosopher?'

'Him. Utterly out of his mind. Wanted me to draw diagrams for him!'

'What sort of diagrams?'

'You don't want to know. Intimate ones!'

'Bless! Has he got his eye on someone?'

'I sincerely hope so!'

It took her a moment to register, and she patted his wrist, throwing her head back in a silent laugh. Matt waited for her to settle. He wanted to be serious.

'Hilary?'

'Mmm?'

'I'm really madly completely head over heels in love with you. I have been since I first saw you. I just . . . knew it.'

She said nothing.

'I don't expect you to say the same. Not for a minute. But – will you just put me out of my misery? When we get back to England – can I see you again?'

She thought about it. Wickedly, she prolonged his agony, then smiled. 'Yes.'

He whooped and tried to hug her to the floor. She pushed him off.

'Wait, though. It's not all sweetness and light. I mean – you're going to have to take it slowly. Like, I'm going to be wading through a lot of shit when I get home.' She looked up to see if he was registering. 'A *lot* of shit. Personal stuff, business things, you name it. I might have to move house. You and I – whatever you and I is – might not survive all that. So all I'm saying is – yes. Yes, yes, yes please! But don't pin all your hopes on me, yeah? I don't know if I feel strong enough for that just now.'

He nodded and gave her his lovely wide smile, eyes

twinkling, happy as anything. 'I know. It's fine. It's beautiful.' He clapped his hands together quickly. 'Thanks. I just wanted a chance with you, that's all.' She kissed him on the nose. 'I'm glad you think I'm worth it. I'll try not to let you down.'

She got up and collected her bags. 'Look. I've got packing and crap to deal with. Shall we meet down at Ayo's? Eightish?'

'I'll be there at six!'

'Enjoy the wait.'

She took off, thinking to herself that the important thing now was to ensure that Shaun didn't find out about Matt. Once again it was all instinct with her. She had no clear idea of what was happening or why, but she was clear on this. Shaun had to be protected.

The moment he sat down with his beer the flies started their assault. One flickered on his face, another buzzed in his ear while a small battalion orbited his head. He tried to ignore them, but the irritating tickle on his skin was too much to bear. He slapped his face, signalling the start of the real game. Now a fly would land on the left side of his face and, as he swished his hand at it, another would land on the other side. As an extra insult, a fat bluebottle settled on his swiping hand. More and more came to hover silently overhead, occasionally dropping down in ones and twos, buzzing infuriatingly in his ear and then buzzing off. He looked at the other drinkers in the beach bar. They, too, were being assaulted by tribes of pesky flies, but they seemed not to notice. They carried on chatting, reading their newspapers, playing checkers. Shaun admitted defeat. He picked up his bottle and loped down to the water's edge where he sat, feet in the surf, enjoying life again. This was him. This was all he wanted. He wanted to sit in peace and watch the world go by and take in whatever lessons were to be learned. He drained his bottle and went over to the water fountain to rinse it and fill it up, ready for his walk. The heat was going to be killing but, first step first, one step at a time, he knew he'd get there.

Hilary found the café by accident. Enjoying the slow walk back to the cliff trail she became aware of her own dawdling. She was in no hurry to get back. That great surge of self-determining power she'd felt was still bristling, but she was enjoying the solitude, too. She didn't have to face up to Matt's puppyish devotion yet, and she found she wasn't relishing the prospect, either.

She stopped to admire the tangled vines and foliage that overran one crumbling building and found a door. Gingerly, she pushed it further ajar and craned her neck inside. It was a long, narrow bar-café, tiled with cool white ceramics, each hand-painted with extravagant flora. At its far end was a small terrace overlooking the sea. One table was occupied by a slumbering old man. The others were free. Although there was no sign of a proprietor or waitress, she felt someone watching her and went through to seat herself. Sure enough, a minute later an old lady – perhaps the sleepy chap's wife – came to take her order. She gave Hilary the benefit of her lurid smile and spoke cheerfully and quickly in Spanish, not seeming to notice or mind Hilary's muteness. She tried to make herself understood, smiling back at the woman and requesting 'cappuccino' and 'gâteau fraise'. Her Esperanto seemed to do the trick. Hilary enjoyed three-quarters of an hour sipping frothy coffee and digging into a deep and syrupy strawberry flan. She watched the holiday vignettes being acted out far away on the beach. Boys were dragging girls into the sea. Mothers were slapping their children's legs to stop them crying – why did they *do* that? Hilary decided there and then that she would never hit a distressed child, no matter how naughty. The thought of herself as a mother galvanised her greatly. It was a million miles away, but it was there. Fuck. One day she would be sitting on a beach like that with kids of her own. And their father. She took in the glorious vista one last time and headed back to the future.

'Typical of fucking Pasternak! He makes a fucking big deal about the last night, gets us all out at this rdiculous time . . .'

'Oh, chill a bit, man! He's right! We should make the effort on the last night!'

'So where is he, then? We've managed to make it to Doctor Fun's end-of-term party! Where's the life and sodding soul?'

Millie, uncomfortable, changed the subject. 'Matt's not here, too. Maybe the two of them had to do something?'

'Matt's coming later. At least he was good enough to tell us!'

Millie snapped. 'Look! Leave Pastie alone, yah? So he isn't here yet! Is it so bad for us five to sit with each other for a short time?'

Tom looked away. Krista whispered to Millie, 'Go easy. He's been crying all day, poor boy!'

Millie smiled and winked at her friend. 'I hope bloody Pastie gets here soon! *I* feel guilty now!'

★

''Nother Depth Charge, please.'

'Blimey, mate! You can knock 'em back!'

The Kiwi barman made an 'I'm impressed' face and started to mix him another one – cider, lager, vodka and lime. He wasn't drunk. He wasn't even tipsy. He wanted to be absolutely sure about this, get the level just right. If he was going to be Doctor Fun – a rampant, lurid, horny Doctor Fun to boot – he had to boost himself up, and he had to get it spot on. There'd be no second chances this time.

He delved for his sachet and eased out two pills, one a little blue diamond, the other an ivory-white Ecstasy. In another sachet was the ground powder of another ten tablets – eight white, two blue. He smiled to himself and crossed his fingers hard. He slipped the blue pill back – he'd have to time that one with immaculate precision – and, waiting until the barman was distracted, used the last of his Depth Charge to neck the 125. Pasternak got up, stretched, left a 1,000 note for the barman who'd been dealing him Jaegermeister, Rocket Fuel and Depth Charges since five o'clock that afternoon, and made his way out of the Robin Hood. He felt brilliant. He knew this was going to be a classic, right down to the choice of venue he'd insisted upon – a flamenco disco in Stars, the open-air club on the beach. It could only be tacky, touristy and fun, fun, fun! He made his way across the Balcón Europa, pausing for one last view of the bay. He picked out the club, just visible way down on the furthest beach. He flicked a look at his watch. Not long, now. He'd told the DJ – and paid him handsomely for – ten o'clock. With any luck the others'd be there now, awaiting his grand arrival. Maybe a slammer or two first, though.

★

Hilary was finding Matt heavy going. He'd insisted upon the restaurant's Dish For Lovers, a giant mixed paella for two which you had to eat out of one big, iron crucible. She was uncomfortable with it all, but tried to allow for his youth and his abundant excitement – but soon she was uneasy with that too. She was cutting him slack she never would have allowed Shaun in the latter months and days.

And he could only talk about them, him and her. The future. She didn't want to clip his wings. He was on a high, the same spiritual lift she'd been rejoicing in herself, and she knew she couldn't expect him to rein it in. So she tried to keep things light and evasive. She touched his hand kindly.

'I don't know, baby. Please don't ask me because, honestly, I can't say. It *feels* final. It's definitely the way we've been heading. But how can I tell you what you want to know? Nobody knows . . .'

He nodded, still serious. 'I'm sorry. I know that. It's just . . . I'm mad on you!'

She tried to laugh it off, then got her say in before he carried on about his devotion to her. 'I'd love to just go dancing, you know? Will you take me?'

He was hesitant. 'Sure . . .'

She guessed that he'd had his heart set on a romantic meal, a walk on the beach and promises of a blissful future together. She wanted the opposite. What Hilary wanted was to postpone all and any thoughts of tomorrow and have some fun, let her hair down.

'Oh, please! It'd be just what I need right now, I reckon.'

He beamed at her. 'I know just the place!'

She tried to fall in with him as he hooked his elbow

around the crook of her arm, and looked deeply into her eyes, eating the paella like Lovers.

Everything about the ride up to Frigiliana told Shaun why he should stay. The pale evening sunshine, the mountain backdrop, the plainsong of the orchard birds – these were the things that had brought him back to life. It was hard for him to correlate that other life awaiting him back home. The other him, scurrying around the neighbourhood at night, vandalising other folks' architectural atrocities, seemed impossible to him now. Had that really been him? Whatever had been eating him, he was starting to get away from it now. Whatever Maggie said, he was going to find a way to stay out here – there could be no question about that. As the birds piped them up to the mountain village, he felt a pleasant wave of familiarity for a place he'd never visited before.

Hilary could tell straight away that they thought she was too old for him. The three girls, in particular, recovered quickly enough and tried to make her feel welcome, but those initial surprised looks and furtive glances as Matt introduced her to the gang said it all. The boys, Mikey and Tom, just stared at first and, when they thought she wasn't looking, waggled their eyebrows at each other and blew out their cheeks. They were saying: 'Bloody Matt! Spawny bastard! He's only gone and copped a randy middle-aged housewife!'

Bastards! She was fucked if she was going to start talking to them about the new Air album or something. She had Evisu jeans back at the apartment, Jil Sander for dressing up. These girls, two of them anyway, had spectacular figures but, frankly, they were hippies.

Scruffs. 'The Dutch Girls', Matt had said, but no way would they have even heard of Ann Huybens or Jorgi Persoons. What gave these lanky hippies the right to look at her like that? She was twenty-fucking-five!

She almost groaned out loud when Matt returned from the bar with champagne, but she checked herself. He was just being nice. She managed to return his besotted smile and rallied herself to clink glasses with the others. She got into a faltering conversation with Anke, conscious of Matt's eyes upon her at all times.

The light was astonishing from their table outside Bar Ingenue. Half of the courtyard was plunged into rusty shadow as the molten-red sun dipped between two peaks. Shaun and Maggie were still drenched in a beguiling, silvery orange twilight, slanting across the table and away to the ravine. The café was backed into a tiny yard adjoining the potters' workshop, with the whitewashed village receding below and the deep scar of the gorge running adjacent. Maggie chuckled at him.

'You look like you're planning a suicide leap!'

He looked up from his reverie and smiled. 'Perhaps I am.'

She leaned across the table and took his hand. 'You were miles away.'

'Literally.'

'Is everything OK?'

He cleared his throat gently. 'Not really.'

She looked sympathetic. 'Bit of a bummer about tomorrow?'

He nodded. 'Specially when you look at all this. I mean, I love it! I *love* it, and I've hardly seen anything yet.' He took a mouthful of beer. 'To think I didn't want to come here . . .' He tailed off and laughed. 'Thought it'd be full of tourists and twats in Union Jack shorts.'

'It is.'

He gulped on his bottle again, thinking hard. 'Well. I like it here, anyway.'

She picked at the label on her Heineken. 'You could stay a bit.'

'Oh, yeah! How?'

She looked up, fixing him with that unreal aqua gaze. 'Stay with me?'

He paused, then batted a hand at the prospect. 'Ah, don't tempt me! You know I can't. What would I do for work?'

She seemed visibly to relax, as if pleased or unburdened by his bringing this to the fore. She took his hand again and tried to make him look at her. 'That's secondary. There's actually no end of possibilities – good things, realistic things, not piecework – if you give it time. The main thing is that you're sure in your heart that you want to give it a crack. If you are, if it's what you want, then . . .'

She shrugged and left it to him. He nodded slowly, first at the table then, raising his head, he met her look. 'It is.'

She couldn't stop the smile spreading over her face. It was, almost, an actual ear-to-ear grin. 'Good. That's that decided, then!'

He started laughing, nervously to start with, then deeply, honestly, passionately. The two of them touched bottles and saluted each other.

Pasternak was starting to get concerned. The tablet was

coming on in gorgeous, reassuring waves. He'd swallowed the Viagra half an hour ago and he was starting to feel a prickly heat in his groin. In the deepest recesses of his cavernous gut, the first pangs of desire were starting to tantalise him. Cool winds seemed to chill his churning testicles, stirring his penis. But he couldn't find the gap in the hedge. He could hear the ululating affray of the party – he could even see Matt, right in the centre of the dance floor, dancing passionately with a cute, pixieish chick. But he couldn't find his hole in the hedge! Flustered now, bothered by the drink and the drugs and the imploding tension of it all, he held his hands up to calm himself and paced the length of the hedge again. It was almost ten. Next track up.

'This is tat!'

'Shh!' giggled Maggie.

'It is, though – it's just pure tat!' said Shaun, drunk, still on a high. The girl in the potters' workshop glared at him. He smiled at her. 'I'm sorry!' he whispered. 'Is this your work?'

She shook her head. Shaun approached her.

'Tell you what. I'll bring you some of my work. It's good. If you like it and want to, you can sell it. Fifty-fifty. What d'you think?'

She examined him. 'I think your work would not be acceptable to my customers. You're right. I display what I know I can sell. A lot of it is shit!'

Shaun grinned at her. 'Sorry! Look what I've started now.'

The girl, flirting with him now, croaked at him in her laryngitic, smoker's voice. 'So you better make sure you're worth it. Don't disappoint me!'

Shaun bowed and went to join the still-tittering Maggie outside.

'I've got a job!' he laughed. 'It's just the small matter of doing it now. Any idea how you make fruit bowls?'

'Doesn't matter, so long as you're a dab hand at painting matadors on them!'

'Or a nice, splodgy, yellow sun!'

They creased up again, guffawing drunkenly as they meandered back down the hill. Even through the drink he was aware that he liked all this laughter. It was new to him. It was something he hadn't really done before.

Millie watched the others forlornly. Mikey and Anke were doing The Bump, as they did to every song they ever danced to. They seemed inordinately fond of each other's bottoms. Tom and Krista stood at the periphery, arms around each other, swaying and kissing. Ah! Holiday romance! It had been denied her, and she felt doubly desperate for the knowledge that she really could have helped Pasternak. Belatedly, she had come to understand his preoccupation. If she could have just got him alone, properly, she could have talked him through it. He had nothing to fear with her. But now, since the time Mikey had tried to humiliate Pastie on the beach, he'd been in hiding. Even the night she'd got into bed with him, he was in hiding. She knew that now. She knew he wouldn't turn up tonight. She sank another margarita and watched the intoxicated Matt. He deserved to be happy. He was a nice guy. His girl, though, his lady friend – she was a stiff. She was biting her bottom lip as she danced, looking at her armpit, watching her feet and screwing her eyes up, trying to do 'funky' in the way of all people who didn't dance. Millie was dying to dance. Maybe she'd just plough up there, on her own. She'd show them how to do it!

'*HEY YOU! DON'T WATCH THAT, WATCH THIS! THIS IS THE HEAVY, HEAVY MONSTER SOUND, THE NUTTIEST SOUND AROUND!*'

She felt the same surge of energetic excitement as everyone else who had recognised the intro. People were nudging one another, aping and grinning, already starting up their own nutty skank dances, losing their footing on imaginary ice rinks.

'*SO IF YOU'VE COME IN OFF THE STREET – AND YOU'RE BEGINNING TO FEEL THE HEAT, WELL LISTEN, BUSTER! YOU'D BETTER START MOVIN' YOUR FEET, TO THE ROCKIN-EST, ROCKSTEADY BEAT!*'

Suddenly, a deranged baby rhinoceros came crashing through the partition hedge, arms above his head, screaming: 'ONE STEP BEYOND!'

He was off! Wild-eyed, ecstatic, punctuating the air with jerky fist and head movements as he acted out the song, Pasternak took over the dance floor, drawing revellers towards him. He was bouncing like a maniac, and everyone was bouncing with him. He was the lord of the dance. The entire club was up with him now, clapping madly, starting to make a big circle around him. Some of the party people recognised him as the kid who'd led the conga at Club Torro the other night. As Millie got closer, she wondered about the scaffolding in Pastie's pants. The notion suggested itself that Pasternak was harbouring an exorbitant erection. She ran to join him in the thick of the mêlée.

★

For the last hour, the music was pure Balearic come-down classics – Billy Ray Martin, José Padilla, the DJ even played 'Spirit of the Age' by Hawkwind. Even Moby's decadently plaintive 'Why Does My Heart Feel So Bad' sounded exultant. Arms around each other, swaying in communion, the Pasternak mob sang their hearts out. Hilary felt a little bit daft.

Millie and Pasternak wandered down to the water's edge. Pasternak skimmed flat stones across the languid surface, knowing that his time was nearly up. Millie came up behind and hugged him.

'Pastie?'

'My scrumptious angel?'

'Can we be together tonight?'

He turned to face her. 'Oh yes! Oh very yes!'

She smiled, worried. 'Be serious. Be yourself. Can we go to your place?'

He leaned down and kissed her. 'I can't wait that long.' He took her hand and led her to a cluster of upturned fishing dinghies. 'Come here.'

Shaun slipped into bed and held her from behind. Nuzzling her back with his chin, he could feel the texture of her skin, coarser than Hilary's silken sheen. Aroused, he began kissing her shoulders, running his fingers along the outside of her arms. The tip of his knob stuck hard into her buttock, jerking up to rest on her hip bone as she turned to him.

'Are you sure?'

'Sure,' he said.

She reached for it, and encircled it with her slender

hand, letting the smallest finger stroke underneath. 'Fuck, Shaun!'

She whispered something passionately, inaudibly, and leaned into him, kissing him slowly and deeply. He tried to push back, tried to master her but she held him firm. 'It's OK, darling. It's all going to be OK.'

Pasternak leaned back against her, exhausted and very, very happy. He'd done it. He could do it. It was fantastic. Millie stroked his damp hair, sticky from the sweat of his exertions.

'Was that your first time?'

He summoned up all the indignant denial he could muster. 'What? *Noooo!* Me? Don't talk mad!'

She smiled. 'It's no big deal if it was.' She nibbled his ear lobes as she spoke. 'You were amazing! The best I ever had . . .'

'Why, madam . . .'

She kissed his neck. 'Do you think you have another one in you?'

'The Love Machine *always* has another one in him!'

She lay back melodramatically. 'Oh, Pastie! Take what you want of me!'

The big lad fell upon her, which must have winded her, though she didn't let on.

'Oh, baby!' groaned Pasternak, producing himself for her. 'Look what you've done to me!'

Hilary dug her fingers into his taut arse as he thrust and grunted and blurted out his adoration for her. She tried to go with it, moaning and bucking back and making the faces, but she wasn't there. It was nothing. Nothing compared to the tremulous, forbidden epiphany of yesterday's rainstorm. That moment, the shocking, slow-motion frame when she knew she was going to do it, was hers to carry with her for ever. This was something else. She lay there and let him fuck her and fuck her and found herself thinking, 'What *is* going on with me?'

A wave of nauseous insecurity came over her with accompanying tears, but she fought it back. She'd get it over with, get dressed, get back and think again.

The Final Day

She wasn't there when he got back to the apartment. The bags were packed, his too – but there was no sign of Hilary. He rummaged through the fridge to see what was left. There was half a litre of full-fat milk that still smelt OK, and a bit of blue cheese. A quick recce in the cupboards soon provided him with a fine and unexpected breakfast of coffee, Special K, bread and cheese. On tasting the bread and finding it fresh enough to eat he actually tilted his head sideways and nodded meaningfully to thin air, just one prolonged 'Mmm. Good!' nod as though he was filming a fresh bread advert.

He kicked around the flat, belatedly guessed that she must be up at reception or by the pool and made his way up to meet her.

Matt awoke with more joy in his soul than he could ever have conceived of. His heart was thumping, the soles of his feet tingling. He couldn't wait to see her again. So it was a shock at first, then a crushing blow for him to find the note she'd pushed under the door. She must have done it some time after dawn because once she'd left last night he hadn't been able to sleep for ages. He couldn't stop thinking about her and hugging his pillow and smiling to himself.

He reread the letter. The words were kind and, in a way, loving. The effect of them was devastating.

Matt darling,

This has been the most wonderful thing. I've tried in my own stupid way to explain that when we get back home things will be very tough for me. So I'd like it best if you could try to be patient. Don't get in touch with me. I promise you I'll call or write when I feel the time has come.

With my love,

Hilary

She had originally written 'when *I* get home', but crossed it out and inserted 'we'. He read it and read it again and he got the message. It was over before it had even begun. He went out on to the balcony, furious tears burning his eyes as he observed the flat sea, wishing he could hurl himself from that very spot, right into the indiscriminate deep. He screwed up Hilary's letter and launched it over the wall. An hour later he was foraging for it in the bushes below, desperate to dredge the text once more for any sign of hope.

They surveyed the broken bed. It wasn't just the bed leg; the baseboard had snapped right across the middle. Millie eyed him lasciviously.

'Oh, Pastie, tiger! Who was an eager little tiger?'

Pasternak gave the bed a final, desultory glance. 'Cheap piece of cack! Look at it!' He picked up a piece of the baseboard. 'Plywood! Did they not realise that this flat would be playing host to one of south Manchester's most energetic performers? Had they not heard tell of . . . Mr Lover Man?'

He made seductive eyes until she laughed, then tossed the scrap of wood away like a frisbee.

Millie took a look at the wreckage and giggled. 'You'd better do *something*! It's only the leg and the underneath part! It's not so bad – maybe if we just put them back together like a jigsaw nobody will notice?'

'Hmm. Worth a try, Watson.'

By the time they pulled the covers back over the bed, it looked as good as new – with a terrible ridge running horizontally across the middle.

Shaun loped up the steps towards the pool, two and three at a time. He was getting the hang of that murderous midday sun – the thing to do was ignore it. Think cool. He followed the narrow path past the limes and the effulgent rhododendrons and started into the last and most abrupt flight of steps.

Up ahead a poor perspiring man, wretchedly pink and visibly turning scarlet as he stood there wilting, was being lectured by a confident fellow in a straw hat. Shaun could see the little man nodding, almost in tears as the sun beat savagely upon his unprotected scalp. He could hear the strident voice of the man in the hat from the bottom of the steps. Everything anyone needed to know about this thin, pompous man was discernible from that persistent, righteous, haranguing voice. Not a syllable of self-doubt had ever crossed his mind. He'd succeeded in drifting through two and a half decades as a building society assistant manager, or an estate agency branch associate partner (assistant manager) safe in the knowledge of two things: he knew what he was talking about; and people wanted to know what he thought. Over the years he had become accustomed to brow-beating reluctant recipients with his unsolicited views, and had grown to like the shiver of self-regard that brought. Here he was, pulverising this humble, gasping, *terrified* new arrival with a scatter of crap information. Shaun approached them. The poor bloke still had his *suitcase* in his hand! His family was probably waiting outside the apartment, patiently waiting for Dad to follow with the key and the bags. Where did this prick in the hat get off, holding up an innocent stranger like that? It was – it was a stick-up! He'd almost reached them, now.

'Of course you pay through the nose in those bars!'

The man in the hat widened his eyes and drooled at his expiring pupil, who nodded and mopped his brow nervously. He was trying not to be rude, but fuck! It was hot!

'Oh yes! He's licking his lips, is Manuel Dago! He's seen you coming! He's saying to his mates – quick! Get the tourist price list up!'

He paused and made his eyes big again. Shaun stopped next to him. The lecturer moved slightly to let him pass, but didn't seem to notice when he stayed where he was. His fanatical eyes stayed trained on his target.

'But go to your *fish*-ermen's bars . . .'

'There aren't any,' said Shaun quietly.

'. . . and you pay the locals' prices! And you have a proper, down-to-earth chat about anything . . .'

'Bullshit!'

'Today's catch. Short-term weather prospects . . .'

'Hot.'

'That's where you want to be, mate. In your fishermen's bars.'

Shaun tapped him on the shoulder. 'Listen, you self-satisfied prick! I live here! There *are* no fucking fishermen's fucking bars! It's a tourist resort!'

The expert turned to Shaun, frightened but trying to puff himself up. 'I'll have you know . . .'

Shaun pushed him in the chest and walked off. 'You won't.'

'Thirty thousand pesetas.'

'What for?'

'Breakage.'

'What breakage?'

'Breakage bed. Is fifty thousand pesetas. Twenty thousand deposit plus thirty thousand.'

'You're fucking joking!'

'No joke. Fifty thousand pesetas.'

Pasternak looked him up and down. 'Who do you think has fifty thousand pesetas left on the last day of their holidays?'

'Not my problem. Take Visa.'

'You can fuck off!'

'Sure. I fuck off with your passports!'

He smirked at Pasternak. Pasternak took a deep breath and started over.

'So, this bed? This balsa wood, mass-produced, self-assembly bed? You're telling me it cost, what? Two hundred quid?'

'Fifty thousand pesetas. Local handcraft bed.'

Pasternak leaned over to him and whispered violently in his ear. 'Fuck you right up your thieving arse! I'm going to the British consul!'

The manager held out the phone, triumphantly. 'Want me to call taxi? Is in Malaga!'

'Fuck off!'

He went back out to break the news. Mikey and Tom, sitting aside with Anke and Krista, heads on their shoulders, didn't seem to take it in. Matt, seething, did. He glowered at Pasternak.

'That's it!' he hissed. 'That is fucking *it*!'

He stormed into the reception area, hurdled the desk with one almighty vault and took the manager by his shirt lapels. He marched him backward into his office and pushed him towards the safe until his spine was digging into its harsh corners.

'Open it!'

'No!'

Matt stuck his nose right into the manager's face. 'Oh yes! You're going to open it! And you're going to give us our passports back like a nice, civilised man. We're good people! We're not yobbos, yeah?' He relinquished his grip, letting the man fall back. He pointed into his chest. 'YOU – are a yob! You're a horrible, beady-eyed robber! I'm giving you a chance to do the right thing, now, before I make a fucking mess of you!'

'I call police.'

Matt picked up the phone and handed it to him. 'As you can see, old chap, I don't really give much of a fuck just now. My advice to you is that you look lively.'

The manager glared at him, his tiny black eyes shining madly. He opened the safe and handed Matt the passports. Matt brushed him down and patted the side of his face.

'Good lad. See you.'

So he told her he was really going to do it – he was staying out here for a bit. She was fine about it – quiet, but apparently pleased for him. She was tearful as he carried the bags up to the top for her. She stopped twice to compose herself, and the second time she just held him tightly. She was trembling. He left his own bag in storage and carried Hilary's to the pick-up point while she went off to make a phone call home.

He padded over to the pool. For the first time since he'd been there, the detergent-blue pool was unoccupied. Bodies were strewn around the periphery, grilling themselves in the gardens, but the pool was empty. One or two women looked up, ogling him from behind the anonymity of their shades as Shaun patrolled the edge of the pool. Invigorated, sexually charged once more, he was aware of their furtive attention. He swished the surface of the water with his toe. It felt good. A sudden surge came over him, the lure of the cool, inviting water. Remembering that he had only briefs under his shorts; knowing that they were unsuitable as swimwear, that they would become transparent and that the lecherous pool lizards would get an extensive view of him, he still could not resist the promise of a delicious cold plunge. He took his shorts off slowly, sizing up his dive. Carefully, he removed his earpiece and slotted it inside his shorts, then made his way to the deep end.

He leaped high, high enough to catch his breath and touch his shins as he shaped to hit the water. There was barely a splash as he arrowed downwards, hitting the bottom of the pool hard with his head and shoulders, almost simultaneously. He came up stunned, ears ringing.

He struggled to the short ladder and held on to it, blinking hard, adjusting his vision and trying to regulate his spasmodic breathing. He was fine. The sunbathers were all spreadeagled, reading their airport pulp, quite unaware of the drama they had just missed. Shaun could have been on the front of that girl's *Mirror* tomorrow. HOLIDAY BRITON IN COSTA DROWNING TRAGEDY.

But he was OK. He felt amazing, actually. He could read the cracking paint, now. The deep end was only 1.8 fucking metres! Signs were nailed to every other tree: DANGER! DO NOT DIVE!

How could he have missed that? He smiled to himself and rubbed his head. Could have been a bad one if he'd gone in vertical. The drone of idle conversation buzzed all around him. Even when they were only arguing about places to eat, holidaymakers' chatter had a certain excitable pitch to it. But something was wrong. Instinctively, Shaun sensed that today's poolside tittle-tattle sounded different. There was an unusual clarity to the din. It took Shaun some time to twig what that was. He could hear, clearly, in stereo. His bump on the bottom of the pool must have done something, released a trapped nerve, whatever. Something had happened to him. He could hear perfectly. And then something else occurred to him. Slowly, talking himself down, trying to quell any sort of nascent hope, he made his way to the bathrooms, praying that his suspicions would be correct. His line of vision seemed less strenuous. He seemed to be finding his range with a lower sight line, and he didn't seem to gravitate upwards, or find himself straining against that. And when he looked in the mirror, he was quite right – the knock had corrected his leering eyeline, too. It was a miracle. A miracle.

'Promise, Pastie? Don't just say it . . .'

'God, Millie – I've never meant anything more

ardently in my ample life! I'll be on the first KLM to Amsterdam on Friday evening. Actually, Easyjet might be cheaper . . .'

She smacked him. 'Just call me, yah?'

'Oooh yah! Most exquisitely, resolutely, definitely yah!'

'Really. As soon as you know what flight, yah?'

'Absolutely.'

He kissed her. She gave him a sultry look.

'And we have the dirty weekend in Old Amsterdam?'

'We have the *sordid* weekend in Amsterdam!'

She wrapped her arms around him and kissed him languorously. Hilary sat on the coach, watching them absent-mindedly through the window. Her seat was right at the front of the coach, away from Matt and the boys. A tap at the window brought her out of her abstract trains of thought. It was Shaun, beaming. He was pointing at himself, making funny gestures she couldn't decipher. He looked amazing. He looked happy, but more than that he seemed fulfilled. He had a serenity that made her, in turn, feel shabby. He blew her a kiss and smiled generously. She tried to smile back, but felt her eyes watering again. She waved weakly to him. He looked fit and lean and beautiful. Her husband, who she was about to leave, was beautiful. She couldn't place it at first, but he kindled sensations from a long-gone past – feelings of desire and anticipation and eager romance, the kind that just unfolds without plans. That was it. Looking at him now was like her first sightings of him, bare-chested up in the scaffolding, then right in front of her that time on the station platform. He bowed theatrically and tried to mime something. The coach driver started up the engine. Panic gripped her, like a first-time flyer, but sustained slapping on the windows from the back of the coach steeled her to the present.

'Pastie! Get on! We're leaving NOW!'

She saw the boy kiss his true love farewell. The hydraulic door swooshed open for him, letting in a delicious gust. He dragged himself up on board, waving to his jeering mates like a returning conqueror. What must Matt be thinking? Poor kid.

Shaun was up against the window, making faces. She managed to summon a childlike laugh from deep within. She looked at the open door. The driver put the coach into reverse and started to back out, slowly. This was it, then. For a suspended moment she thought she was going to dive off the coach, grovel in the dust and beg him to come back with her. She recovered quickly from that, and felt strong. She was alone now, but she was in control. She still had the power. The coach reversed so that it could turn and change direction. Hilary stopped looking at Shaun and watched the driver fight to manouevre the big, clumsy bus. Who could know what was around the corner? Anything can happen. Nobody knows anything.